JEROME CHARYN was born in New York City in 1937. He has taught at Stanford, Princeton, and Rice, and is currently a visiting professor of English at the University of Texas. He is the author of fifteen novels. THE EDUCATION OF PATRICK SILVER is the third volume of the acclaimed Isaac quartet, which also includes BLUE EYES, MARILYN THE WILD, and SECRET ISAAC. He is also the author of THE FRANKLIN SCARE, available in an Avon edition, and the SEVENTH BABE, available in an Avon-Bard edition. THE CATFISH MAN will soon be published as an Avon-Bard title. His most recent novel is DARLIN' BILL.

Other Avon Books by
Jerome Charyn

BLUE EYES
THE FRANKLIN SCARE
MARILYN THE WILD
SECRET ISAAC

Coming Soon

THE CATFISH MAN

THE EDUCATION OF PATRICK SILVER

JEROME CHARYN

 A BARD BOOK/PUBLISHED BY AVON BOOKS

AVON BOOKS
A division of
The Hearst Corporation
959 Eighth Avenue
New York, New York 10019

Copyright © 1976 by Jerome Charyn
Published by arrangement with Arbor House
Publishing Company, Inc.
Library of Congress Catalog Card Number: 76-8633
ISBN: 0-380-01698-2

All rights reserved, which includes the right
to reproduce this book or portions thereof in
any form whatsoever. For information address
Arbor House Publishing Company, Inc., 235 East 45 Street,
New York, New York 10017

First Avon Printing, August, 1977
First Bard Printing, January, 1981

BARD IS A TRADEMARK OF THE HEARST CORPORATION
AND IS REGISTERED IN MANY COUNTRIES AROUND THE WORLD.
MARCA REGISTRADA, HECHO EN U.S.A.

Printed in the U.S.A.

"An Irishman is never drunk as long as he can hold on to one blade of grass and not fall off the face of the earth."

—from a plate on the wall of the Bally Bay bar, Christopher Street

PART ONE

1

Patrick Silver left the baby in the lobby of the Plaza Hotel. The baby, who was forty-four, sat in an upholstered chair, with his knuckles in his lap. His name was Jerónimo. A boy with gray around his ears, a Guzmann of Boston Road, his education had stopped at the first grade. He lived most of his life in a candy store, under the eye of his father and his many brothers. But the Guzmanns were feuding with the police. They couldn't protect the baby on their own. They had to put Jerónimo in Patrick Silver's care. Patrick was his temporary keeper.

Jerónimo had blackberries in his head. With a carpet under his feet, and candelabra around his chair, he was thinking of the Guzmann farm in Loch Sheldrake. It was the blackberry season, and Jerónimo wanted to stick his fingers in the briars and drink blackberry juice. But he was a hundred miles from

Loch Sheldrake, waiting for Patrick Silver in a hotel with rust-colored wool on the floor.

Patrick Silver rode the Plaza elevators in a filthy soccer shirt. The elevator boy was uncomfortable with a giant who stank of Dublin beer. Silver had a ruddy look. He came to the Plaza without his shoes. He was six-foot-three in simple black socks.

Patrick began roaming the corridors of the third floor. Chambermaids pushed their linen carts out of his way; a shoeless man was anathema to the maids, who glanced at Patrick's socks with their noses hidden in the carts. They returned to their business once Patrick knocked on a door. He muttered three words. "Zorro sent me."

He walked into a room that seemed uncommonly small for a hotel that had elevators with gold walls and carpeting that could hide a man's feet. A girl stood behind the door in a sweater that once belonged to Jerónimo; it swam around her shoulders, but it couldn't tamper with the shape of her breasts. Patrick didn't have divided loyalties. He was paid to protect the Guzmanns and all their interests. Still, he wasn't a man who could ignore the impression of nipples inside an old sweater.

The girl smiled at Patrick's socks. She'd heard of this crazy bodyguard who lived in the basement of a synagogue and wore soccer shirts and a holster without a gun. She liked the scratchiness of his face, the white hairs on his knuckles, and his imperfect nose. She was Odile Leonhardy, the teenage porno queen, and she admired men with enormous beaks.

The Education of Patrick Silver

She had moved uptown, taken a room at the Plaza, to break into legitimate films.

"Where's your yarmulke, Patrick Silver?"

"In my pocket," he said.

"Why don't you put it on?"

"I wear it when I'm praying, miss. Or when I have the shivers."

"What happened to the baby?"

"He's downstairs."

"Is it safe to leave him alone?"

"Miss, no cop would ever lift him from the Plaza Hotel. I ought to know. I was a detective for thirteen years."

"Don't call me *miss*. I'm Odile. Didn't Zorro tell you to bring Jerónimo to me?"

The girl was confusing him. "No. Zorro went to Atlantic City. He asked me to visit you and say he'd be gone for a while."

"What's he doing in Atlantic City? Zorro hates the ocean. Did you ever see him take off his shirt?"

"He didn't go there for a swim. He has some business in New Jersey."

"Good for him. Now do your job, Patrick Silver, and show me Jerónimo."

Did she intend to play clap-hands with the baby? It wasn't Patrick's affair. He ducked around the chambermaids' carts and pulled Jerónimo out of the lobby. What kind of power did Zorro have over the girl? She unbuckled Jerónimo's belt and growled at Silver. "Wait outside."

Patrick was becoming a middleman in his old age

11

(he'd be fifty in another eight years). The Guzmanns had made him into an Irish pimp: he was the one who steered Jerónimo to Odile's bed.

Patrick had to listen to a whore's music; he couldn't stray from the door. Odile mumbled "Jerónimo, Jerónimo," and the baby began to groan. He didn't cry out of displeasure, Patrick understood.

The groans stopped coming through the wall. Jerónimo couldn't have been inside more than three minutes. His belt was buckled when Odile brought him out. She had the same rumples in her sweater. "Tell Zorro Odile wishes him luck in Atlantic City."

"I'll do that, miss."

Patrick took the baby's hand and held it on their stroll through the corridors. Jerónimo had a wet palm. He walked with great swipes of his head, his shoulders dropping on the downswing and his chest whistling as he dragged Silver to the elevator cars.

Jerónimo exhausted his Irish keeper. Patrick had to fight for air. The two ancient boys stepped into the elevator. Passengers stared at them. Patrick and Jerónimo had huge tufts of gray-white hair; their thick clothes had a winter smell; the giant with the soccer shirt didn't believe in shoes.

They walked out of the elevator holding hands again; the baby had Patrick by the thumb. He led his keeper beyond the edges of the Plaza awning and into a damp July.

There were quiffs at the terminal, quiffs and spies, with the imprint of shotguns under their dashikis, police aerials climbing up their backs, newspaper stuffed in a brassiere; behind the bushy wigs they were blond "angels" from the First Deputy's office. They belonged to Isaac Sidel. Their Chief had lost his war with the Guzmann family, a tribe of Bronx pimps and policy rats, Marranos from Boston Road. Papa Guzmann and his five sons, Alejandro, Topal, Jorge, César, and Jerónimo, had irritated the Chief by crossing the Third Avenue Bridge to run a whore market in the middle of Manhattan. Isaac the Brave couldn't trap César, who was called Zorro in the Bronx, with his gang of baby prostitutes. So the Chief had himself pushed out of the First Deputy's office, disappeared into the Bronx, and emerged as a factotum to Papa Guzmann, on Boston Road. But his nearness to the Guzmanns brought him few advantages. He came out of the Bronx with a tapeworm, a black tongue, and no arrests.

The blond "angels" were going to avenge their Chief's disgrace. They scoured Port Authority for hints of Zorro and his brothers. They would have broken Alejandro's neck, drowned Topal's brains in a toilet bowl, shoved nickels and quarters in Zorro's eyes.

They didn't catch a thing. Zorro stepped around the dashikis in silk underpants. His face was smeared with the wax of a melted brown crayon, and he carried a straw suitcase like the Chicanos who were smuggled into New Jersey every summer to farm for sweet potatoes. His brother Jorge had come with him. The melted crayon left tiny bits of rubble under Jorge's ears.

The brothers climbed aboard a coach with ancient rattan seats. Zorro had a Bronx banana for his brother and a suitcase full of apples from his father's orchard. The apples were slightly bruised. The Guzmanns had picked them just before Isaac's friends in the FBI sneaked onto the property with an acetylene torch and put an end to Papa's farm.

The boys endured rattan spears in their buttocks for Papa's sake. They were going to visit a bagman named Isidoro, who was one of Papa's distant cousins.

The bagman owed his existence to Papa. He was starving in a shanty outside Bogotá when Papa rescued Isidoro and delivered him to a candy store in the Bronx. This candy store had a multiplicity of lives: it was the Guzmanns' headquarters, hospital, bedroom, and numbers bank. Isidoro would have been content eating bitter chocolate and growing bald in the candy store if Isaac hadn't come along. Unable to corrupt any of Papa's five boys, the Chief whispered in Isidoro's ear. He frightened the poor *bogotano,* advising him what the Manhattan police did to bagmen. "They'll drill holes in your tongue unless I help you, Isidore. You have no future here."

He turned Isidoro around with this and other blandishments. The bagman became a spy for Isaac. His revelations were small; he would only sell the Chief isolated scraps of information. After Isaac shucked off the candy store, the bagman skipped to Atlantic City. The disappearance of Isidoro and Isaac made Papa scratch his head. He began to guess the cozy relationship between his cousin and Isaac the Shit.

The brothers arrived at the old terminal on Arctic Avenue. Jorge was having hunger pains. He clutched

The Education of Patrick Silver

his belly and made pathetic squeals, searching for candy vendors who didn't exist. Zorro had no more bananas in his pocket. But he had to quiet Jorge; squeals from a man with a twenty-inch neck would call attention to them, place the Guzmanns in Atlantic City. "Jorge, don't cry. You'll get candy on the beach."

They took the Arkansas Avenue route to the boardwalk, stopping at a Hadassah thrift shop to buy Jorge a hat that would keep the sun out of his eyes. They passed a row of forlorn hotels crouching near Pacific Avenue, with little beaten porches and stoops, and old men behind the screens. The great mildewed cupola of the Claridge blinked at them from South Indiana. The smell of suntan oil oppressed the brothers soon as they struck the beach. Without the shelter of Arkansas Avenue, they had to suck hot wind.

The curve of the boardwalk made Zorro grumpy. He couldn't go very far on wood that bent away from his feet. He led Jorge to a fudge shop. Jorge smiled at the conveyor belt that carried roasted peanuts from the window to an oven deep in the shop. A puppet with lively hands was mixing fudge in a copper bowl behind the peanuts. The puppet's bushy hair reminded Jorge of his older brother. "Jerónimo," he grunted, forgetting his belly for a minute. He didn't want fudge—black, white, green, or yellow. Zorro had to buy him red-hot dollars, candy fish, and almond macaroons.

They crept over the hump in the boardwalk, avoiding the linked trolley cars that were swollen with passengers in banjo hats who licked on miniature bottles of rum and laughed at Zorro's coloring. "Follow us, Crayola Face." Jorge would have bumped the trolleys, spilling every banjo hat under the boardwalk, if Zorro hadn't restrained him with a thumb in his pants. "Papa warned you not to feud with idiots. We'll lose track of Isidoro. Brother, remember what Isaac did to us. He tried to kill Jerónimo. He took our country home."

Jorge hurled pieces of macaroon at the trolley cars. He grunted curses that only the Marranos could have understood. He spoke in muddled Portuguese. But he didn't knock fenders off the cars. He fell in behind his brother. People stared at them from the sun decks of monstrous stone hotels that pushed into the edge of the boardwalk. The rust on the hotels' copper roofs had turned a slimy green. The stone walls of the sun decks were splintering under the surface. Jorge followed the lumps in the nearest wall.

The impurities in the stone shimmered under the soft bill of his cap. Jorge would have dawdled with a hand on the wall, but Zorro steered him away from the sun porches. A tug of his pants brought him inside a gypsy booth that was nothing more than an ugly gash in the wall. The word "Phrenologist" was painted over the booth in a pretty yellow. It frightened Jorge, who couldn't read thick words, although he was smarter than Jerónimo. Jorge could iron a necktie, utter whole sentences, and pee with fortitude into the heart of a toilet bowl. Like all his brothers he had no specific birthday (his father was superstitious about such events), but he was a summer child, born in January, during the dry Peruvian season, just under forty years ago.

Jorge felt a breeze on his neck in the gypsy cave. A pregnant woman sat near the entrance of the booth in a man's undershirt. She welcomed the brothers into her cave with a powerful yawn, wrinkling her undershirt and sending fissures through her belly. Zorro didn't interest her. She liked small ears on a big head. Jorge had to stoop for the gypsy. The woman breathed into his scalp. Without fingering Jorge she could interpret the design of his earlobes and the magnitude of bumps on his skull. "This boy covets women," she said. "Be careful with him. His knees aren't strong. He's going to fall."

"Fine," Zorro said. "Terrific. I'll watch my brother's knees." He dropped five dollars into the gypsy's undershirt. "Madame Sonia, save your forecasts. Our religion doesn't allow us any future. We're Catholics in a prehistoric way. We love Jesus but we don't have much use for his mother. So don't expect pity from us. My father's getting lonely for his cousin. Where's Isidoro? You're supposed to be his landlady now."

The *bogotano* was short on brains. Half of Papa's runners and pickup men vacationed on the boardwalk between Texas Avenue and Steeplechase Pier, because Miami was too far away. The runners had seen Isidoro with the pregnant witch.

"Sonia, don't be mean. You counted the ridges in my brother's hair. He's getting homesick. Can't you tell? He has gas pains whenever he leaves the Bronx. Where's Isidoro?"

Jerome Charyn

A boy sprang out from behind the witch's chair. He put a small revolver against Jorge's head. He had crooked teeth, Zorro noticed, and the revolver's taped barrel shivered in Jorge's ear. "That's my son," the pregnant gypsy said. "He listens to me. He'll blow your brother's face off, I swear. Get out of Atlantic City."

Jorge didn't turn glum. A gun in his ear couldn't make him freeze. He swallowed a candy fish and stuck two fingers around the cylinder of the boy's gun. The flight of Jorge's hand puzzled the witch; it seemed idiotic to caress a gun with two lazy fingers.

Zorro rubbed his cheek. The Marranos despised firearms (guns were for city bandits and cops like Isaac the Toad), but Zorro understood the tenacity of his brother's grip. He dug a fingernail into the witch's belly. "Bring me Isidoro."

The boy hissed at Zorro and tried to curl the trigger; he couldn't get the cylinder to spin. Jorge's two fingers had smothered the action of the gun. The witch rolled in her chair. The Guzmanns had to be less than human, creatures with stinking souls; who else would eat lead bullets with the pounce of a thumb? "Misters, don't hurt my boy."

The gun disappeared into Jorge's sleeve. The gypsy wagged her head. Only men who drank the boiling piss of Christian-Jewish saints could be such strong magicians. Sonia had heard of the Marranos, who could call upon Moses of Sinai, Jesus, Jacob, and the kings of Babylon to protect them. She led the brothers out of the cave and into the dense grass of her private lot, a wedge of ground behind Pennsylvania Avenue. There were no boardwalk trolleys in the witch's grass, just the signboard of an old restaurant, The Merman's Roost, pieces of tin meant to look like a gondola, or another long ship, rusting on the ground, the gondola with its edges bitten off and enormous pocks in its middle.

Jorge was confused by a gondola in the grass. He could shred his pants crossing a boat that had teeth in its two gigantic ears. Zorro had to walk his brother over the signboard, knee by knee. The rust disfigured Jorge's shoes.

The gypsy brought them to a bungalow at the end of the lot. The brothers couldn't find a serviceable door. They had to crawl through a hole in the porch screen to get into the gypsy's house. The bagman didn't give them any trouble. He yelled to Zorro from the kitchen. "César, what can I make you? I miss your father's tea. I don't have the patience to say prayers over the kettle. Not like Papa."

"Isidoro, my tongue isn't dry today. I'll live without your tea."

The bagman shuffled through the kitchen in his pajamas. Zorro's spite was gone: he shouldn't have been harsh with his father's cousin. The Guzmanns drank deep red tea with Isidoro. Jorge burnt his fingers on the glass. Isidoro allowed himself a timid smile. The crypto-Jews of Spain, Portugal, Holland, Brazil, Peru, and the Bronx could only enjoy scalding tea; the fire in their gullets told them they were still alive.

With red tea inside him, Zorro's anger slowed. He had finances to discuss. "Isidoro, Papa owes you a hundred and seventy dollars. I saw it in his ledger. How should it be paid? To the gypsy and her son?"

"Half," the bagman said. "Half to Madame Sonia, and half to the orphans' home on Stebbins Avenue."

"Isidoro, you know the fools who administer that place. Your charity will go into some rich doctor's pocket." The bagman's puffy eyes clipped Zorro's arguments. He penciled in a figure on his shirt cuff, where the Guzmanns did most of their arithmetic. "Eighty-five dollars to the orphans of Stebbins Avenue," Zorro announced. Then he and Jorge hugged Isidoro; the three of them swayed near the gypsy's stove. The brothers hadn't lost their affection for the *bogotano*.

They held their embrace while Jorge sniffled and the bagman inquired about Jerónimo. "The baby's in good hands. Papa hired a bodyguard for him. An Irish baboon." Zorro began to smell Isaac on the bagman's pajamas. He finished the embrace.

"Isidoro, you shouldn't have taken Isaac the Shit for a sweetheart. Why didn't you sing to a different cop? . . ."

Jorge clapped his elbow under the bagman's mouth. Isidoro didn't writhe against Jorge's chest. His eyeballs didn't have a bloody expression. The veins didn't rise on Isidoro's cheeks in slow, horrible clusters of blue. The bones cracked once behind his ears, and the bagman was dead.

A truck would arrive late in the afternoon. The Guzmanns weren't sacrilegious people. Provision had been made for Papa's cousin. He wouldn't have to lie under Jersey soil. The truck would transport him to the

The Education of Patrick Silver

Guzmann cemetery in Bronxville, where a company of mourners would rip their clothes in Isidoro's behalf and wail until the sky got black.

The brothers left the bungalow through the same hole in the screen, crossed the rusty gondola, and came out of the gypsy's cave. They locked themselves in a toilet on Steeplechase Pier. Zorro spilled articles out of his suitcase. Apples, two bandannas, skirts, a blouse, high-heeled shoes. Jorge left the pier with the two bandannas on his head and apples in his blouse. This was the way Zorro would sneak him back to their father's candy store. Isaac the Shit had cops everywhere on Boston Road. Only niggers, children, and girls in bandannas were safe.

Jorge grew somber under the scarves, blouse, and skirts. He pushed the apples down to his waist. He hobbled on the boardwalk. Zorro couldn't get to Arkansas Avenue without buying more candy fish for his brother.

2

"The dark bottles, Sammy, if you please. In the usual tub. I've a thirst on me could destroy a hippopotamus."

Patrick Silver drank his Guinness warm. It came from Dublin in tiny bottles that were packed religiously behind the counter. The Kings of Munster couldn't fail its principal client. An Irish bar on Horatio Street, it was never out of Guinness.

Silver needed his twenty nips. He would stumble into the Kings of Munster exhausted from his tribulations at the synagogue. The barman had a pitcher waiting for him after evening prayer. It was Patrick's lot to raise a minyan (a quorum of ten upright Jews) for his shul. He had a curious affinity for capturing Jews. He would

Jerome Charyn

roost on the steps of the synagogue and chirp at passers-by, whether infant, man, or boy. "Are you Jewish, sir?" If you hesitated for a moment you were lost. Patrick would swipe at you from the stairs, clutch an arm, and haul you in. He could carry two men or three boys in a single trip. Having Jerónimo made it easier for him. He would stick a prayer shawl over the baby's head and include him in the minyan. Jerónimo's mewls didn't upset the minyan's droning music. If he was short one Jew, Patrick had his prayer book. He would wrap it in the fringes of his shawl, pronounce a blessing, and the prayer book became Patrick's tenth man.

But the strain of so many minyans was beginning to tell on Patrick, who had to mind the synagogue and the baby. So he sat in the Kings of Munster on the stool he preferred, away from the window and the dog shit on Horatio Street that traveled so fast in July; it was dangerous for an Irishman to be out of doors. "God bless," he said to barman Sam before drinking from the pitcher.

Silver nursed his bottles. He didn't grow a Guinness mustache until the fifth bottle had been poured. The Kings of Munster wasn't a bar for guzzlers. Patrick nibbled on the beer, scooping in the bitter foam with his tongue. He loathed American beer, pissy blond water that could have been brewed in a bubble-pipe. Silver was a Guinness child, born with a black bottle in his mouth. His da, who made pencils in Limerick until a mad priest chased out all the Jews, took him to the Kings of Munster when he was a month old and sat him on the bar. Patrick learned to crawl this way, on a bumpy sheet of iron that was galvanized with whiskey and Dublin beer. He didn't have to sneak his nose into a gentleman's pitcher. He drank his Guinness right off the bar, warmed over with a slight taste of zinc.

By the twelfth bottle Patrick had mustaches on three sides of his face. He began to croon his father's songs about the witches, giants, toads of Limerick, and the burning of Wolftone Street. Pissed in the head, with Guinness blowing out of his ears, he saw a wicked Chrysler pass the Kings' window three times. Patrick spit into his hand to scare off any avenging angel who might be hovering near Horatio Street. He knew the owner of the car, and its principal passenger. He said goodbye to Sammy, picked up his britches, and hobbled out of the bar.

It was treacherous to go around the bend of Abingdon Square in stockings alone. But Patrick couldn't wear shoes. Leather bands on his feet gave him ungodly blisters. As a cop he'd been at the mercy of his superiors: the PC wouldn't allow unshod detectives near his office. Patrick had to stuff cotton balls through the neck of every shoe in his closet. He walked on cotton for thirteen years, howling at the number of blisters he endured. The medics at Bellevue had never heard of a cop with such sensitive feet. Patrick avoided the chiropodists and their talk of miraculous foot powders. He would hop about in agony when he had to chase a thief.

Now he was watching for dog shit. He curtsied up

close to the benches of Abingdon Square park, suspicious of the gray areas between lampposts. He was a bit nearsighted in the evening. He didn't notice the baldish head inside the park until it hissed at him. "Silver, come here."

Patrick groaned. "I could tell that was you in the First Deputy's car. Why the fuck are you following me?"

The man on the bench was Isaac, Isaac the Brave, who'd left his ruddy cheeks in the Bronx. And most of his handsomeness. He had splits in his forehead that wouldn't go away in the dark. His jaw sat crookedly on the spindles of his neck. A Guzmann must have slapped back Isaac's teeth.

"Patrick, it isn't fair for you to ignore us. Commissioner Ned was a mother to you. He raised you at Headquarters. You ought to visit him once before he dies."

"If I ever went near Headquarters, you'd put me in chains and clip off my toes."

"Your head could stand some clipping ... where's Jerónimo?"

Patrick began to falter in his black socks. He knew all the First Deputy tricks. Isaac hadn't waylaid him in the park just for a chat. These were clever people. Isaac's "children" had to be poking about, angelic boy detectives who wouldn't have been ashamed to sack an old shul. Patrick had to run home before the angels kidnapped Jerónimo. But the Guinness had clubbed

The Education of Patrick Silver

him behind the ears. He couldn't march with two tangled legs.

"I asked you where Jerónimo was."

"Isaac, me darling," Patrick said, putting on his best Irish, a brogue that had been nurtured in a Bethune Street synagogue, around a dwindling band of "Hebes" who hadn't seen Ireland in sixty-nine years. "The lad's asleep. We had a feast today. Chocolate pie from his father's candy store. He likes to nap after a big meal."

"Is there any blood on his fingers?"

"Why?"

"Because he's been playing on the roofs."

A young boy had been found on the roofs above Charles Street with a ripped neck. Someone had crayoned his eyes, ears, and lips in dark red. Homicide squads from Manhattan South were scouring the district for possible child murderers.

"Isaac, you're full of barley. The lad never goes higher than the ground floor. He can't function near windows and fire escapes. Wouldn't I know? We've been stuck together for a month. I'm with him every minute."

Isaac came out of the shadows. There wasn't a single curl on his face. He had rough patches where his sideburns used to be. He seemed bereft without his tufts of hair. But he could still hiss at a man.

"No wonder Jerónimo lives with you. That's a perfect couple, you and the baby. Patrick, you're the dumbest detective in human history. The First Dep was your survival kit. You would have drowned years ago without his devotion. If you can account for Jerónimo minute by minute, where is he now?"

Black fumes bubbled out of Patrick's nose: he was snorting air and Guinness at Father Isaac. "Didn't I say the lad was asleep?"

He managed to push off, get himself beyond the park and Abingdon Square. His legs were carrying him. His knees held. He could ignore Isaac's whistles. "Get a pair of shoes, you son-of-a-bitch." He was over the gutters, onto the curb of Bethune Street. "If you don't deliver Jerónimo to me, I'll put rat poison in your beer. Your lungs will smoke. Silver, stay off my streets." He didn't have to position the fall of his toes. An Irishman always landed well. Patrick couldn't miss. He banged into the shul, striking one of the awning rods with his skull. "Jesus," he muttered, with a lump on his head. He went under the stoop, fumbling for his latchkey. Pissed blind, he couldn't contend with a keyhole.

"God of Esau," he said, "come to me." He cursed Jacob and Rebekah, who had swindled Esau out of his birthright. Esau was a hairy man, like Patrick Silver and Jerónimo. But Patrick had no birthright to lose. His father left him a prayer shawl with plucked tassels and the obligation to preserve a synagogue for Irish waifs.

The key turned in Patrick's hand, and the synagogue unlocked itself. He stumbled towards his room, afraid to peek for Jerónimo. He heard snores behind the wall. He thanked the God of Esau for preserving hairy men. He opened the door. Jerónimo was in Patrick's bed, under a summer blanket. The blanket rose with the thrust of his snores. The baby drooled in his sleep; a piece of the blanket was wet. Patrick didn't care. He'd slept in the baby's spittle before.

3

Isaac the Brave drank his slug of castor oil and went into the craphouse. It was part of his Wednesday morning routine. The craphouse belonged to Presbyterian hospital. Isaac had to donate specimens to the tropical disease lab. Technicians examined his stool once a week. The Chief had a worm in his gut, spiteful and intelligent, eight feet long, with hooks and many suckers.

Isaac's worm was the prize of tropical diseases. Doctors and technicians couldn't remember another worm that thrived so spectacularly in a man. They would shoot dyes into Isaac to fluoroscope the worm.

"Inspector Sidel, are you sure you haven't been to South America? This isn't 1905. Nobody picks up a pork tapeworm in Manhattan any more."

The Chief began to dread his walks to the craphouse. He left the hospital weakened by castor oil. But he didn't have to crawl to Headquarters like a wounded bear. His chauffeur would bring him downtown.

Detective-sergeant Brodsky was waiting outside the hospital in Isaac's enormous Chrysler. He couldn't warm to the Chief's new look. Isaac had gone into the Bronx with curly sideburns. He came out with ashes in his nose, his Moroccan suspenders ruined: the supports were crusted with layers of white chocolate. His teeth were brown. His hair had the disordered feel of plucked chicken feathers. The Chief was all gray. Six Guzmanns in a candy store had sucked on his marrow. It couldn't have been a small winter for Isaac. Papa Guzmann didn't allow hibernations on Boston Road.

The Chief stumbled over to the Chrysler. "Brodsky, a little boy was killed on Charles Street. They brought him down from the roof. He had red shit on his face. Isn't that familiar to you?"

Brodsky was trying to draw the shivers out of his neck. Isaac had startled him. Brodsky could live with grunts, but he hadn't expected whole sentences from the grizzly bear.

"Isaac, it can't be the lipstick freak. Didn't Cowboy put him away? The guy is in the Tombs. A Puerto Rican dressmaker."

"Cuban," the Chief said. "And he never made dresses. They were dolls."

The bear grew silent again. Brodsky maneuvered the Chrysler with a thumb. He felt some wind behind his ears.

"Are you going to take Cowboy's word that our freak is still in jail?"

Chief of Detectives in the City of New York and president of the Hands of Esau (a brotherhood of Jewish cops), "Cowboy" Barney Rosenblatt was Isaac's great rival at Headquarters. Cowboy could have squashed an ordinary police inspector, but Isaac worked for the most powerful cop in North America, First Deputy Commissioner Ned O'Roarke. The First Dep had a tumor in his throat. He wasn't supposed to be alive. Cowboy couldn't depend on the ravages of any disease. While Commissioner Ned sat in the First Deputy's chair, the Chief of Detectives had to curtsy to Isaac the Brave.

"Isaac, why should Cowboy lie to us?"

"Because he's a prick."

The chauffeur was stuck. Who could question the logic of a bear? "A prick," he muttered. "Definitely." And he drove into the First Dep's private ramp.

Isaac had to shuffle around an army of clerks. Headquarters was picking itself out of Centre Street. The City had built a huge red brick fortress for the Police Department near City Hall. The cops would have their own plaza and a building that was impregnable to thieves, revolutionists, and crumbling rock. Even with the Guzmanns pulling on his brain, Isaac was disheartened by the move. He didn't want air-conditioned chambers and a memory bank that could give you the size of a criminal's smelly blue sock. No data system could trap Papa Guzmann, or explain why Jerónimo wore earmuffs in June, July, and August.

Isaac had one of his "angels" call the Tombs. This angel reported back to the Chief. "Isaac, they lost their records on Ernesto, the lipstick freak. They don't know where he is."

"Then let them dig. If they can't locate the cubano in five hours, I'll have to bite the warden's ass. You tell them that."

This wasn't the first prisoner who'd disappeared from the Tombs. A Corrections officer would arrive in a few days with evidence that a crocodile had swallowed the lipstick freak. There would be drawings of Ernesto inside the crocodile's mouth, and a pocket saved from the freak's chewed-up pants. Isaac went in to see Commissioner Ned.

Four sergeants patrolled the First Dep's anteroom. Isaac had put them there. They discouraged crime reporters, nosy clerks, and police captains who thought they could improve their lot with genuflections to a dying Irish commissioner.

The First Dep sat in the corner, with a blanket over his knees. His green eyes were licked with dull yellow spots. Cobalt treatments had burnt his vocal cords and left him with a hoarse whisper. His yellowish eyes were a poor clue. O'Roarke's mind didn't drift, no matter how much of him had been eaten away. He ran Headquarters from his little chair, supervising the slow exodus from Centre Street.

His eyebrows didn't bunch for Isaac. His wrists crept under the blanket. "Where's Patrick Silver?"

Patrick had once been the darling of Ned O'Roarke.

The Education of Patrick Silver

They were Limerick men, worshipers of the river Shannon. Patrick's touch of Judaism couldn't disturb Commissioner Ned. Irish Jews had lumps of Catholic tissue under their foreskins. Only Silver had crazied himself drinking Guinness and Irish coffee. He'd shot too many chickenshit thieves. He'd gone into pimps' lairs waving his .45, with Guinness coming out of his eyeballs. The PC had to take his gun away. Silver was made into a clerk, a member of the rubber-gun squad. He jumped the First Deputy's office, leaving his pension behind.

"Patrick's in his synagogue, Commissioner Ned. Asleep. I've sent a few kites down to him. With regards from you and me. They landed in Silver's park. My detectives have more kites to deliver. They'll revive the sleeping beauty."

Isaac left O'Roarke's private room with a twitch in his gut. It could have been the worm. Or an outbreak of jealousy. Those Irishers liked to cuddle one another around the ears.

There were hyenas in the hall. Herbert Pimloe skulked with Cowboy Rosenblatt outside the First Dep's office. Pimloe worked under Isaac. He was O'Roarke's deputy whip. But he'd attached himself to Cowboy. The moment Commissioner Ned faltered in his chair, they would push down on Isaac's scalp and tear the skin off his face.

"Cowboy, what happened on Charles Street? Tell me about the mutilated boy."

Cowboy played with the studs on his holster and ignored the Chief. Isaac crept in front of Pimloe.

Jerome Charyn

"Wasn't there lipstick on the little boy's cheek? It sounds like an old story."

"Herbert," Cowboy said, leaning into Isaac to nudge Pimloe's arm. "It's the Rasties, aint that right? They're into cult murders this time of the year."

Headquarters was frightened to death of the Rastafarians, a community of black Jamaicans who worshiped King Haile Selassie and wore their hair twisted into long "dreadlocks" to resemble a lion's mane. The Rastafarians had settled in Brooklyn and the Bronx, and were busy making war on these boroughs and murdering themselves.

"Cowboy, this is a different cult. The Rasties wouldn't take a nine-year-old onto the roof. It's the lipstick freak, or one of his brothers."

"Yeah," Cowboy said. "Jerónimo. Maybe I ought to send the homicide squad down on Papa's baby. Who knows? All the Guzmanns could be lipstick freaks."

"Don't laugh. You wouldn't have any dead boys if the Guzmanns stayed in Peru."

"Isaac, I'm sick of your theories about Jerónimo. That boy's a white-haired dummy. Just because you hate the Guzmanns, it don't mean they produced the freak. The freak is in the Tombs, and I put him there."

"Cowboy, guess again. Ernesto is missing. Somebody walked the dollmaker out of the Tombs."

Isaac didn't send for his chauffeur. He crossed the Bowery with his own feet. No one waved to him from the barber colleges and the candy stores. Once Isaac had been the only bishop of the Puerto Rican-Jewish

The Education of Patrick Silver

East Side. Merchants would rush out of their stores to kiss the bishop's hand. A nod from Isaac meant prosperity. The old *dueñas* of Eldridge Street could walk with their purses dangling from their thumbs. They had big Isaac to retrieve any articles stolen from them. But Isaac had fallen out of touch with the landladies, grocers, and pensioners of his bishopric. The Guzmanns had pecked under his sideburns and devoured the white meat in his head. Isaac stumbled through the East Side like an unbrained bear.

He stopped at a dairy restaurant to guzzle five bowls of split-pea soup. Isaac had to feed his worm. The countermen weren't impressed with Isaac's devotion to split peas. They waited for the bear to climb off his stool. Isaac could corrupt a place with the sweat clinging to his nose.

The Chief had more than split peas on his mind. He was looking for his girlfriend Ida, who was head cashier of the Ludlow Street café. He couldn't find her around the cash box, the butter tub, the vegetarian salamis, or the stove, where Ida loved to roll square pancakes for the blini and blinchiki that were a special feature of the house. Isaac made inquiries from his stool. The countermen shrugged at him. "Isaac, honest to God, she vanished one day. Don't think she wasn't loyal. She stared out the window month after month."

"Myron," Isaac said, with a finger inside the counterman's shirt. "You'd be bankrupt without that girl. The blintzes would crack if she ran too far. So tell me where Ida is?"

"Home," the counterman said. "She's fixing her trousseau."

"What trousseau?" Isaac said, with his lip stuck out.

"She has a suitor . . . he's here. In the restaurant."

Myron pointed to a man with plastic on his sleeves who sat eating mushrooms off the edge of his thumb.

"That's Luxenberg . . . our accountant."

Isaac went across the street and knocked on Ida's door. She swallowed hard after she recognized the Chief. Ida wasn't malicious. She offered tea and sponge cake to the cop who had deserted her. She wouldn't spoil the occasion with shrill cries. How often does a man come back from the dead?

"Isaac, believe me, what's nine months between friends? But couldn't you have sent me a postcard from the Bronx?"

"Police business," Isaac said, with sponge cake in his mouth. "My own daughter didn't know. Ida, I was caught in a freeze. The Guzmanns dipped me in cold chocolate. They put spiders in my hair. They gave me a worm."

"Isaac, who are the Guzmanns that they should do such disgusting things?" Ida watched him lick some honey off the side of his spoon. The Guzmanns, whoever they were, hadn't robbed him of his old habits. The Chief loved to sniff for honey. "Isaac, I'm engaged."

"They told me at the restaurant. Luxenberg. An accountant with plastic cuffs. Ida, does he wear plastic when he pees?"

Ida walked into the kitchen. The Chief followed her.

The Education of Patrick Silver

He began taking off her clothes. He didn't rip Ida's blouse. He was diligent with all her buttons. He had Ida's skirts and summer bloomers on the kitchen table without scratching her legs. He didn't need a blanket under him. He could grovel on Ida's linoleum. She coughed when Isaac licked the gulley in the middle of her chest. She felt the bear's hot nose in her belly. Ida understood. He was sniffing for his honey jar. He stirred, pushed his head away. The Chief forgot to undress himself. His pants came down. He crept into Ida.

The bear was miserable. He copulated with his skull against the wall. Only a retard could be blind to Ida's motives. She was afraid of the Chief. The girl had deep grooves in her mouth. She went walleyed under Isaac: her pupils shrank inside her head.

Isaac bit his tongue. The doctors had told him about the vague discomforts a worm could bring to a man. Isaac cursed the doctors and their fluoroscopes. The worm was eating him alive. Its armored head pinched and scraped his gut. He swore to Jesus he could feel the cocksucker twist around. The worm was conspiring with Ida to agonize the Chief. He slid out of her, clutching his pants. He knew a cashier's tricks. The girl suffered Isaac on top of her to deflect him from her suitor's plastic sleeves. Ida gave her own honey to the bear, so he wouldn't go back to Ludlow Street and rage against Luxenberg and the dairy restaurant.

Isaac stole out of the kitchen. His knees were stamped with the print of Ida's linoleum. He fled across the Bowery with sludge in his heart. The Chief had lost his old avenues of comfort. The bishopric was gone.

Herbert Pimloe was a cop with a Phi Beta Kappa key. He'd dreamt of Oliver Cromwell and Thomas Hobbes years ago in Harvard Yard, under a wet coat and a miserable wool hat. Pimloe rejected the mundane boundaries of a Harvard degree. He had contempt for lawyers and other government boys who longed to smell an ambassador's breath and die for the diplomatic corps. Pimloe became a cop in New York City.

He married a girl from Chappaqua. He moved to Brighton Beach. He had three boys, who inherited Pimloe's gruffness and Pimloe's brains, and grew obsessed with the shape and gold color of a Phi Beta Kappa key. Pimloe patrolled the streets of Brooklyn in a blue bag. He didn't mouth idle bits of knowledge at his precinct. But he couldn't escape from Harvard Yard. A young inspector in the First Dep's office picked him out of Brooklyn. The inspector was Isaac Sidel. Isaac wanted a patrician on the First Deputy's lists, a boy with a gold key.

Pimloe carried fingerprint cards up from the basement. He brought sandwiches to the Irish commissioners. "Find my shoelaces for me, Harvard. Get me some ink for my pen. Harvard, where the fuck are you?"

He became the deputy whip, sweeping up after Isaac, coming down on cops whose ears had begun to corrode. Whole precincts were afraid of Isaac. No one could figure where he would pounce. A deputy whip

The Education of Patrick Silver

lacked this option of surprise. Familiar at the stationhouses, much more visible than the Chief, Pimloe was the man you hated.

He survived on swift elbows and memories of Thomas Hobbes. He annexed himself to Isaac's rival, Cowboy Rosenblatt. With Cowboy's help he would crawl around Isaac and sit in the First Deputy's chair.

Isaac was a tainted man. Feuding with the Guzmanns, he'd crippled himself. He could no longer inherit O'Roarke's chair. The Irish commissioners would never trust a cop who jumped into the Bronx for a tribe of Marrano pimps and penny bankers.

Pimloe stood under a designated tree in Central Park (close to South Pond), and dreamt of the First Deputy's chair. He had a sour time. There were twenty inspectors at Centre Street who could outrank a deputy whip. Cowboy would have to push him over their heads.

Meanwhile Pimloe kept to his tree. He had an appointment with Odile Leonhardy, the retired porno queen. Odile wouldn't take him up to her room at the Plaza Hotel. She claimed that a cop could scare off film producers. She was dying to break into the movies. So she picked a spot that couldn't endanger her; it was a tree with a split trunk that gave Pimloe an uncompromising view of the Plaza. She wanted the cop to eat his heart out.

The grayish walls of the Plaza turned light pink at the end of July. It was a color that reminded Pimloe of frozen entrails in a fish store, and blooded-out meat. The whip was growing somber. Pimloe was jealous of all the producers who mixed with Odile. He imagined men without their clothes, making Odile into another Merle Oberon, while she sat on someone's hairy knee.

"Herbert."

Pimloe saw a lump of sky through sunny leaves, and a heel broader than the back of any yellow duck in South Pond. The heel dangled right above Pimloe's nose. Odile was inside the fork of a powerful branch. Pimloe didn't have to peek around the hump of her platform shoe. The girl wore a dress that was totally transparent.

"Couldn't we sneak into the Plaza?" Pimloe begged from under the limbs of the tree. He had a horrible lust for Odile. "How much would a few minutes cost?"

The whip could have frightened her; he had titles to throw at Odile. Herbert Pimloe would be the new First Deputy the minute O'Roarke fell off his chair.

"I'll buy you a dress at Bloomingdale's," Pimloe shouted into the tree. "Come down."

"No."

"Then tell me what you want."

"Pommes frites."

Pimloe began to shake; Odile would lure him into the Café Argenteuil on Fifty-second Street, where she would gobble French fried potatoes that cost two dollars a sliver. Pimloe would have raided Bloomingdale's to glut Odile with clothes. Material draped on her body gave pleasure to the whip. But he wasn't going to make a pauper of himself for *pommes frites!*

"Odile, cafés are out. It's too early to eat French

fries. What about some whiskey? I brought my flask along."

He offered Odile a drink. Whiskey fumes crept up the tree. Odile wouldn't surrender to a puny silver bottle that was going black from the grease on a policeman's thumb.

The whip's knees came together in one bitter knock. His shoulders drooped. He spilled whiskey on his pants. "Okay," he said. "Pommes frites."

The tree shivered once. A pair of veiled buttocks slid off the branch. Pimloe heard hissing in the leaves. Odile was on the ground. She stood higher than the whip in her platform shoes.

She was the miraculous lady of Central Park, a leggy creature without a hint of underwear; all the hermits and banditos from around the pond left their hiding posts to gaze at Odile. The swing of her legs out of glorious hip sockets caused each of them to choke on his tongue. She had the stride of an ostrich. She covered merciless territory with the flick of her knees.

Pimloe could taste the ligatures of Odile's spine. The dents in the small of her back gave off a salty perfume. He'd have to slip away from Brighton Beach to marry Odile. Pimloe could fight off the wrath of those Irish superchiefs. He'd wait until they crowned him. Then they'd have to kneel to Commissioner Pimloe. The First Dep could have any number of wives.

4

The cab driver had two ninnies in the back: a grayhaired infant and a huge Irishman in stinky socks. He'd picked them up at Abingdon Square because it was a slow day and he couldn't afford to select his passengers. He shuddered when he heard the giant mention Boston Road. "Excuse me, I couldn't find Boston Road in a hundred years."

"We'll teach you how to find it," Patrick Silver muttered, with a knuckle in his toes.

A piece of scratched leather stuck out of Patrick's soccer shirt, but the driver couldn't see the bulge of any gun. What kind of mick wears an empty holster? A crook from Boston Road? Or a cop with a fascination for leather? The driver knew all the precincts from

Jerome Charyn

Chinatown to High Bridge, but he hadn't met scruffy cops like these: gray-haired boys in charity suits. The small one kept shoving caramels into his mouth. The driver humped down into his seat to absorb the shock of exploding caramels.

Patrick chose the Willis Avenue Bridge. The driver began to sulk. The black water under his cab swelled up like overcooked blood. The Harlem could never be a genuine river in his estimation; a toilet for the Bronx, it ran on hot piss, carrying blood and garbage into the sea. A boiling piss-hole and two imbeciles with gray tufts behind the ears had cut him off from Manhattan.

They passed over the skeleton yards of a freight terminal on the Bronx side of the bridge. They were in Mott Haven, on the lip of an old industrial region, cluttered with warehouses and an uncertain railroad that seemed to exhaust itself near the water, with pieces of track about to spill off the end of the borough. The warehouses leaned into the bridge like huge, prehistoric teeth.

The driver felt much safer moving across the bones of Southern Boulevard, with street after street of rubble. The whole Bronx could vanish in front of his eyes. Why should he care?

Little bodegas with tin walls began to crop up around Boston Road. The driver saw a flood of green cars. He smiled as he recognized the outline of institutional green: only a cop sitting under a blanket would ride in a big green boat. Could the imbeciles in his cab be part of the same team?

The Education of Patrick Silver

"Jesus, tell me, who are you guys staking out? Dope fiends, niggers, voodoo men?"

The mick made him stop in front of a miserable candy store. It was a matchbox of dying tin and wood, wedged into the wall of a tenement with disconnected fire escapes; struts were missing from every ladder.

An old man came out of the candy store wearing the traditional smock of a petty entrepreneur. His thick body was completely uncombed. His eyebrows grew wild on his head. A furrier would have envied the hair on his knuckles and his wrists. The driver couldn't believe that this old man had created the fuss of cop cars on Boston Road.

"Shove off," the mick said, slapping a twenty-dollar bill into the driver's pocket. The driver wagged his head. He was in a nothing borough, outside a candy store that sat in the ruins, surrounded by a squatters' army of cops in green boats. He waved to the infant, Jerónimo, anxious to get out of firing range. "Thanks," he crooned to Patrick Silver. "Thanks."

Papa Guzmann waited for the cab to leave before he hugged Jerónimo. He'd been itching to touch the boy, to fondle the ears of his oldest child, but he wouldn't hop towards Jerónimo in the presence of strangers. The Guzmanns were a sensitive race. Papa could tolerate the big *irlandés*. Silver worked for him. And Silver didn't have a devious smell. Papa judged you with his nose. He could pick out a lying, sinful creature with his very first snuff.

He brought Jerónimo into the candy store, away

47

from the smog of Boston Road. Jerónimo began to mewl for his brothers. Two of them, Topal and Alejandro, arrived in their pajamas from the back room, which had bunk beds and a crib (for Jerónimo) and served as a dormitory and a way station for cousins from Peru and pickpockets from Ecuador and Miami who came under Papa's largesse. The two pajama boys disappeared inside Jerónimo's embrace, but they couldn't stop his mewling. Jerónimo licked their foreheads with a creamy tongue while his face grew wet from prodigious, penny-round tears. The baby could have raised his grandfathers out of hell with the energy he provided. César and Jorge were missing. Jerónimo called for his youngest brother. "Zor-r-r-o."

Papa couldn't help his child. Zorro had been exiled from the candy store by Papa himself. It was Isaac's fault. The Chief had produced a moronic twelve-year-old girl who swore in front of three assistant district attorneys, and a Manhattan judge that César Guzmann, alias Zorro, alias the Fox of Boston Road, had captured her off a Port Authority bus, sodomized her, and sold her into prostitution. Papa realized the falsity of this claim. No Marrano would ever sodomize a cow, a girl, or a horse. Papers were prepared for Zorro's arrest. Now Isaac's killer squadrons sat on Boston Road with bench warrants in their pockets. Zorro would lose his scalp if he came near the candy store.

Jerónimo bent behind Papa's malted machines, looking for César and Jorge. He put his fist through comic book racks stuffed with school supplies, Valentine boxes, and pornographic displays. Papa had dioramas

The Education of Patrick Silver

that told the story of abductions in Egypt, wife-swapping among the Eskimos, concubines in Sardinia, brothels in Peru. Jerónimo didn't enjoy cardboard women poking out of a corrugated landscape. He bruised their heads with a fist.

"Zor-r-r-o."

Papa offered him a chocolate egg, pink licorice, some runny marzipan. Jerónimo scorned such food. It was only after he scraped the walls of Papa's dormitory, with his nose under the beds, to prove Zorro wasn't available to him, that he settled down to eat. He had a brick of halvah, white chocolate that couldn't be broken without a hammer, a pound of Turkish delight, and an egg cream Papa made with a pint of syrup and two quarts of milk.

Nothing he ate or drank could put the baby to sleep. He was restless in the candy store. Papa had given him away. He lived in the basement of a synagogue now with Patrick Silver. He shuffled through the dormitory with his belly in his hands, but he couldn't get familiar with his old crib. He took his naps in Silver's bed.

The baby's nervous walk saddened Papa. He muttered words with Silver to take his mind off Jerónimo's estrangement from the candy store.

"Do the cops haunt your synagoga, Irish?"

"Not at all. Moses, Jerónimo is safe with me."

Papa dug a finger into his smock. "Isaac has his spies. Couldn't he plant one inside the congregation?"

"Moses, not to worry. We haven't had a new face at

the shul in forty years. Anyhow, you can't hide too many pistols under a prayer shawl."

"Irish, take him home," Papa said, squinting at the baby. "He's outgrown the people here. None of my other boys has ever been to a Jewish church."

"Should I bring him next week?"

"No," Papa said. "Isaac's children are getting too close. We'll have green sedans on my counter in a few days."

Silver understood Papa's bitterness about the green sedans. Until Isaac's "children" arrived on Boston Road, Papa's candy store had been the premier numbers bank in the east Bronx. But Boston Road was dead. Papa's runners had to eat their own policy slips. The green cars followed them everywhere. They couldn't accept a nickel play from the hog butcher on Charlotte Street without interference from the cars. Detectives hissed at them and banged on the hog butcher's window. The runners came to Papa with a twitch in their eyes. Papa had to let them go. "Chepe, here's a fifty. Don't be bashful. You have an aunt in New Jersey, no? Visit her for a while. I'll tell you when to come back."

Father Isaac had turned the candy store into a tomb for Guzmanns. Jorge was the only one who crept in and out. Papa would pin a grocery list to his shirt (Jorge couldn't remember the names of different breakfast cereals), and send him to the bodega on the opposite side of the street. The cops were frightened of Jorge. He was a boy who could pull a detective out of a car and shake the clothes off his body. Jorge had the

The Education of Patrick Silver

squeeze of a python. It wasn't fair. Isaac's "children" had a complete armory in their cars. Blackjacks and clubs would have disintegrated on Jorge's skull. Shotguns were inadequate. A detective had his limits. You couldn't blow a man's head off in the middle of Boston Road.

Papa launched the baby with a fresh supply of caramels. "Jerónimo, listen to the Irish. He's your father now. Don't forget to wash your mouth. If you misbehave, the Jews will clip your hair." The baby kissed his brothers and left with Patrick Silver.

Patrick wasn't a jittery person. The cop cars that bumped around his feet couldn't make him scramble for the sidewalks. A detective sergeant taunted Patrick and the baby from the lead car. "Silver, stop wiping Papa's ass. Give us the dummy, and you won't have to slave for the Guzmanns any more. I can promise you your gun and your shield."

Patrick slapped the sergeant's fender. "You can have him, but not alone. The lad goes with me." He opened the door and got in with Jerónimo, pushing the sergeant to the edge of his seat. The sergeant broke his discomfort with a smile.

"Silver, I could drive you straight to Headquarters with the siren on. Isaac will know what to do with the dummy."

"Me and Isaac have the same rabbi. His name is O'Roarke. The First Dep watches over me. He's a clansman of mine. Our people are from the kingdom of Limerick. O'Roarke will smash your fingers if you whistle in my face. We'll go to Bethune Street, thank you. Hurry up. I'll be late for evening prayer."

Papa wasn't blind. He saw the baby sitting in a police car. It didn't worry him. Silver's nearness to the police was beneficial to Papa. An ordinary goon couldn't have preserved Jerónimo's life. Papa had no choice. It was the synagogue or the candy store, and Papa didn't trust himself. He had swallowed llama shit in Peru, drank the blood of a mountain goat to fight starvation, but Jerónimo couldn't survive on Boston Road. Isaac would have seized him from the candy store. Papa couldn't keep that son-of-a-bitch out of the baby's crib, no matter how many cops the Guzmanns happened to kill.

Isaac had been born into this world to plague Guzmanns. That's what Papa believed. Every man has a personal devil, according to Marrano law. Isaac was Papa's devil. What other explanation could there be for a cop who tossed his badge out the window so he could come to the candy store with tales of banishment from the Manhattan police and dig into the flesh under Papa's heart. Moses could have turned him away. But he followed the instincts of his forebears, the crypto-Jews of Portugal, chamberlains and monks who wouldn't have let a devil out of their sight. It was better to hug Isaac and sniff the color of his urine, a pale yellow and blue.

Papa should have whispered in Jorge's ear; Jorge knew how to clog a devil's windpipe. Only Papa was wary of cops. He'd killed another policeman years ago

The Education of Patrick Silver

and had to flee Peru. He wanted Isaac to suffer a more natural death. The Guzmanns had been sophisticated poisoners for a century and a half. But Papa didn't have to cultivate toxins for Isaac. He sat Isaac at his table, fed him pork, tripe, and black pudding. No devil could survive Guzmann food. Papa and his boys had enough acid in them to purify a field of wormy pudding (the family lived out of a garbage pail during Papa's first years in the United States).

Isaac's skin began to turn. His sweat was dark green. His ears had ugly secretions in the morning. The Chief was dying bit by bit. A fingernail would come off. His bushy sideburns, the envy of Manhattan, thinned to lusterless shreds of hair. He tramped Boston Road in a constant state of dizziness. But Papa couldn't get him to fall down. He escaped the Guzmanns by walking out of the candy store and returning to Manhattan.

And Papa suffered ever since. He lost his hegemony in the Bronx. It did him little good to bribe the cops of his borough. The green sedans didn't come from there. Isaac held all the ganglions at Headquarters like puppet strings. He could tug at the Guzmanns from Centre Street. Papa shut the candy store in May and retired to Loch Sheldrake, where he had a small farm with orchards and a country well. But those ganglions could shake a blackberry bush. Isaac reached into Loch Sheldrake. He got the FBI to burn Papa's farm. The fuckers would have kidnapped Jerónimo if Papa hadn't hid the baby in his well.

He relied on Patrick Silver now. Papa had no one

Jerome Charyn

else. If Patrick failed him, devil Isaac would hurl the baby into the sinking lime under Headquarters. Marranos couldn't sleep in an unholy grave. That's why Papa kept a cemetery in Bronxville. The baby would scream for a thousand years without Marrano earth in both his eyes. Could a father ignore such screams? Papa would haunt Manhattan borough like a golem, slaying policemen until Isaac disinterred his boy. He shuddered to think of the consequences. Manhattan would swim in cops' blood. On the death of his sons Papa had no mercy.

A broadnecked bandanna girl hobbled into the candy store with a blind man clutching her arm. The blind man had yellow cheeks, brittle glasses on his nose, and a white cane that was longer and thinner than a fisherman's rod. The bandanna girl unraveled her clothes. Jorge emerged. Papa hugged his middle child. He threw Jorge's bandannas, skirts, blouse, shoes, and apples (meant for tits) into a barrel under the soda fountain. He scowled at the blind man.

"Zorro, you know how much Isaac admires you. Why did you come here?"

Zorro snapped the eyeglasses off his nose and got rid of his white cane. "I wanted to sit with my brothers." He had candy fish for Topal and Alejandro, and purple fudge from Atlantic City.

Papa couldn't control his youngest child. The Fox of Boston Road had to spite those green cars and peek into his father's candy store.

"You missed Jerónimo," Papa said. "By two minutes."

"I saw him," Zorro said. "Did you expect me to stand in front of Isaac's car and bow to Jerónimo? How's Patrick Silver?"

"Why don't you visit his church on Bethune Street? You can ask him yourself."

Zorro mashed his teeth. "I don't trust that Irish prick. He came out of Isaac's belly. Just like Coen."

"Coen never harmed us. And where would we put Jerónimo if we didn't have the Irish?"

"Jerónimo could stay with me."

"Wonderful," Papa said. "He'll sleep in a telephone booth with his brother. He'll live on whores' snot. You'll wash his handkerchiefs in the rain. Pretty. Very pretty."

The malteds Zorro drank as a child must have shrunk his ears. He still had a grudge against Manfred Coen. Coen was dead. They grew up in the candy store, Manfred and Zorro. They were schoolmates. They did their lessons with ice cream in their cheeks. They fed pigeons on Boston Road. They picked bugs out of Jerónimo's hair. But Coen went to work for Isaac, became a blue-eyed cop, and lost his life in a crazy accident. He caught a bullet in the throat at the end of a Ping-Pong game. Patrick Silver used to chase bandits with Coen. He was one of Coen's many partners until the Police Commissioner took Patrick's gun away.

"Zorro, the Irish loves Jerónimo. Don't abuse him. Where's cousin Isidore?"

"He's safe, Papa. Our friends carried Isidoro out of Atlantic City."

"Did you get mourners for him? I don't want my cousin to remain unblessed."

Zorro was a blind man again. He put on his brittle eyeglasses and found the thin white cane. "Papa, would I spit on cousin Isidore? I gave him more blessings than he deserves. It cost me a hundred bills to find a cantor who would pray for him."

The Fox kissed Jorge, Alejandro, and Topal, muttered a goodbye, and started to leave the candy store, tapping with his cane.

"Zorro, be careful," Papa said. "The dark glasses don't mean shit. Police cars run over blind men too."

Zorro didn't wave. Hunching his shoulders, he sniffed the air, and stepped into the gutters of Boston Road.

5

The Congregation Limerick sits on Bethune Street between a Chinese laundry and a hospital for cats and dogs. No one can remember its proper name. In the delicatessens and bars around Abingdon Square it is known as the Irish synagogue, or Patrick Silver's shul. A crumbling brownstone, its stained-glass windows are shuttered with pieces of cardboard, and its awning, extravagant in 1930, is now an ugly stretch of cloth.

This is a suffering shul. It exists without a president and a governing board (the elders of the synagogue, a disabled troop of bachelors and widowers, do not have the energy to govern). It is attached to no other congregation in the world. It doesn't commune with the chief rabbi of Dublin, or the old synagogues of Cork. No rabbinical council in the United States can claim any ties with the Irish synagogue of Bethune Street. It has no sisterhood to perform charities in Greenwich Village and search for odd bits of stained glass that are missing from the windows. It cannot afford a cantor's fee; no one comes here to lead the chant for the dead.

Bethune Street has a rabbi, Hughie Prince, a tight-lipped man who was never ordained. Ask him where he studied. Hughie didn't come out of a rabbinical college. The elders chose him because he was the single person among them who understood a word of the Mishna and the Gemara. Hughie brought *talmud* to the Irish synagogue, limiting his pronouncements to five or six sentences a week about ths laws of dispersion as they applied to Limerick Jews. He cuts glass for a living, and you can only find him at the synagogue mornings and evenings. Most of the time Hughie is out repairing windows; you have to go up and down Hudson Street screaming "Rabbi Hughie Prince," if you expect any religion from him.

Patrick Silver runs the shul. He's the unpaid "beadle." He won't allow besotted Irishmen to piss in the study hall. He feeds the poor (gentile and Jewish beggars can always get a sandwich from Patrick in the shul's tiny kitchen). He settles arguments between parishioners by thwacking both parties on the left ear. He goes into the streets to collect bodies for Rabbi Prince (without Patrick's minyans the shul would forget to pray). He travels through the synagogue with a shillelagh of a broom, slapping mosquitoes off the wall, clubbing rats out of the damp holes in the cellar, lopping off the head of any evil nail in the pews that

The Education of Patrick Silver

might scratch the pants of unsuspecting widowers, poking for weak spots in the chapel's crooked ceiling to prevent the synagogue from falling on Hughie and the sacred scrolls, banging dirt from the underside of the awning, scaring off burglars and bill collectors, and occasionally sweeping the floors.

Even when he had his gun, Patrick lived at the shul. He would shuffle from Bethune Street to the First Deputy's office, with bottles of Guinness in his shirt. Most of his salary went into the shul. Congregation Limerick was a firetrap. Inspectors and City marshals received their monthly "tithes" from the shul and ignored the rumblings in the walls.

Then Patrick lost his gun. A few days after he quit the police, building inspectors arrived with flashlights, complaining about mud in the cellar and rats nesting in the pipes. Patrick needed a fresh supply of cash. He had nothing but muscles to sell. No white man would hire him. The gangster families of Atlantic Avenue and Mulberry Street were suspicious of Patrick Silver. They couldn't understand the pedigree of an Irish Jew. They figured a big commissioner still kept him on a string.

Patrick had to go into Harlem and become the bodyguard of a black policy bank. This nigger bank liked the idea of a giant with a yarmulke in his pocket. Patrick's soccer shirt was soon a familiar item on St. Nicholas Avenue. The bankers grew fond of him. They introduced him to an Abyssinian shul near Mt. Morris Park. Every congregant at this shul was considered a rabbi. Patrick read *torah* with the black rabbis of Mt. Morris Park and discussed the laws of Moses with them. The rabbis had their own Book of Genesis. Jacob was white, the rabbis said. But Moses and Esau were Abyssinian. "Rabbi Silver, you're as black as any of us." Patrick couldn't agree or disagree. Didn't some of the Irish say that St. Munchin, the first bishop of Limerick, had come out of Africa with a colony of leprous Jews?

Patrick's seat in Harlem didn't last. The nigger bank had to let him go. The cops downtown were flying kites over Seventh Avenue. Policy runners were being nudged off the street. "Shit," the bankers said to Patrick. "Somebody's got it mean for you. Irish, we can't afford you any more." The bankers didn't leave Patrick stranded without a job. They tossed him to the Guzmanns.

That's how Patrick inherited Jerónimo. But the boy came with a dowry of sores. The morning after Patrick returned from Boston Road, a squad of Isaac's "children" descended upon the shul. Nine blue-eyed cops broke into Patrick's room and caught him sleeping with the baby (the cellar room couldn't hold more than one bed). Patrick reached for his shillelagh with his prick out. He wouldn't wear pajamas at the synagogue. Jerónimo remained under Patrick's summer blanket, his face wet from the energy of a fourteen-hour sleep (he'd been dreaming about his brother Zorro). All the blue-eyed cops had Detective Specials in their hands. They stayed clear of Patrick's enormous broom. Their spokesman, a detective-lieutenant with a blond mustache, began to bray.

"St. Patrick, we haven't come to harm you. Praise

The Education of Patrick Silver

the Lord, we're on a peaceful mission. The First Dep is in the hospital. He had a hemorrhage in the middle of the night. I didn't see him but I hear the blood poured out of his neck. There's a priest with him now. The Father's laying holy oil on old Ned while they're pumping new blood into him. Isaac doesn't want him to die without a peek at your face. So don't cause trouble for us, St. Patrick. We're taking you to the hospital one way or another."

Patrick kept his chin on the broom. "Isaac must be shaky if he had to send nine dogs like you."

"He's conservative," said the mustache (Lieutenant Scanlan), with an eye on Jerónimo. "He knows how ferocious a Jewish saint can get. Isaac has faith in numbers. He thought nine of us would be enough to discourage you. St. Patrick, do we have to wreck your little church?"

"Put your guns away. They stink of metal. And close your eyes. Me and Jerónimo have to dress."

Isaac's "children" wouldn't slap their guns into their holsters, or shut their eyes; they watched Jerónimo's balls as he wiggled out of bed. The baby climbed into underpants that came down to his knees. He wore sweaters rather than a shirt, and his trousers had a shrunken seat. He pulled earmuffs out of his pocket, winding the tin band around his elbow. Patrick had to lace his shoes.

The cops giggled at the two gray-heads and prepared to march them out of the synagogue. "Not so fast," Patrick grumbled. "This aint an amusement park. Scanlan, you'll have to lend me a few of your pretty boys. They'll be darling Jews for half an hour. Isaac won't object. I'm not leaving until I find ten live customers."

He pushed through the detectives and stationed himself at the doorway. Six old men stood in the corridors. Stalwarts of the congregation, they hung out on Bethune Street and were the hub of Patrick's minyans. They carried their prayer shawls in soft velvet bags, these friends of Patrick's dead father. Patrick shouted into the corridors.

"Where's Hughie?"

The old men shrugged at him. "Hughie's shitting somewhere, or chopping glass."

But Hughie appeared. He had a warped back from bending over glass so long, and his fingers were nicked from all his cutting tools. He wouldn't wear the traditional fur hat (with pigtails) that identified the rabbis and wise men of Eastern Europe. And he didn't have a yarmulke done in gold to set him apart from ordinary men. He came in a simple cap, threadbare at the rims, with a crown that was permanently collapsed; it had goggles sitting on the bill that kept glass splinters out of his eyes. Hughie wouldn't remove his goggles inside the shul. He saw no contradictions between *torah* and his trade. You couldn't be a good rabbi and a bad glazier, according to Hughie. He cut glass with the fingers of Benjamin, Jacob, and Elijah on his wrist.

Hughie stared at the detectives and their arsenal of guns. "Patrick, chase them out. They don't belong in a synagogue."

"Not to worry, Rabbi. I invited a couple of the lads to pray with you."

Three detectives were left behind. They hiked upstairs with Hughie and the six old men of the shul. They had to pass the kitchen, the study hall, the toilets, and the winter room (open to beggars from November to March), before they got to the chapel. The detectives snickered at the circumstances of these Limerick sheenies, who prayed in a dunghill. It was the most abominable church they had ever stumbled upon. The pews were shoved into the corner like a line of bishops in ragged clothes; the carpets running from the pews had trails in them that could have swallowed a yarmulke, or a mouse. The women's gallery, two gnarled porches over the cops' heads, had been stripped of all its benches, since women no longer came to the synagogue.

The chapel itself was in ruins. The furniture made no sense: silk rags on a broken closet, a platform with feeble bannisters, a chair nailed to the wall. They asked Hughie about the odd dip of that chair.

"Rabbi, do you drop your sinners out of the bucket?"

"That's Elijah's chair. It faces north, to Jerusalem, Baghdad, and the Irish Sea. That's the path Elijah takes when he zooms over the world. Next time he comes down from heaven, he'll sit with us."

Isaac's three "children" couldn't believe the gullibility of Irish Jews. Donkeys out of Limerick. (Scanlan, their boss, was descended from Donegal Bay.) Limerick had always been the idiot's house of Ireland.

The sheenies began distributing prayer shawls, and each detective was obliged to bury his head in a huge linen shawl with broad stripes and primitive tassels that were no more than knotted strands of cloth. The detectives were called to the praying box (that miserable platform at the center of the shul), with Hughie and the six old men. They stood on the bottom step, trapped in Patrick's minyan. They heard sounds that froze to the linen on their heads. The minyan bellowed and moaned like a company of sick cows. The detectives would rather have prayed among Rastafarians, or another lunatic cult, than fall into the maw of a prayer shawl.

The Irish synagogue was only three blocks from St. Vincent's hospital, but the lieutenant had to take his fleet of cars. He couldn't walk Silver and the dummy Jerónimo across Abingdon Square with guns in their backs. Silver was practically a saint on Bethune Street. Idiots would pour out of the bars to retrieve him from Scanlan, who would be charged by some civilian board with kidnapping church officials. So Scanlan kept them off the streets.

He was sick of Guzmanns. He'd been exiled to the Bronx since June, riding up and down Boston Road like a Mississippi pilot. You could ground yourself in a pothole, disappear into the crumbling gutters. A Bronx detail couldn't guarantee your life. He would have been happy to get rid of Jerónimo, make one less Guzmann in New York, but he couldn't move on the baby with Patrick Silver in the car.

The Education of Patrick Silver

"St. Patrick, should we stop for a lick of ice cream? Jerónimo won't survive the morning without his chocolate mush."

Silver wouldn't talk. He sat with his knees against the door, thinking of Commissioner Ned. He wasn't a total ignoramus. He could have gone to Headquarters from the synagogue, or the Kings of Munster, and visited with O'Roarke. He didn't forget the route. Only his legs wouldn't carry him there. The First Dep had half a floor to himself. Patrick dreaded those rooms. They'd nurtured him for over ten years.

Patrick was the mad cop of Centre Street, a Limerick lad with a yarmulke, the only kike who belonged to the Shillelagh Society (a brotherhood of Irish detectives). He brawled with the Shillelaghs, whored with them, met them at weddings, wakes, and society dinners, but Patrick didn't go to Mass with his brothers, or follow them on retreats. He pissed into a bottle at Headquarters. He napped with a yarmulke over his eyes. He broke away from an assignment to nab victims for morning and evening prayers. No one but Patrick had a key to the shul. Field commanders couldn't punish him for his lapses. Commissioners were forced to smile at him. Patrick Silver had the biggest rabbi in the universe: First Deputy O'Roarke.

O'Roarke was a distant cousin of the priest who had thrown all the Jews out of Limerick in 1906. He didn't share his dead cousin's belief in sheenie devils. He had a primitive love of Irishmen that could tolerate any church. He knew the family names of Patrick's congregation. He had dialogues with Hughie Prince at the

Irish synagogue, or Hughie's shop, on the question of messiahs, golems, and antichrists. He'd been to chapel with the Limerick Jews. He had a skullcap in his desk. He adored Patrick Silver and kept him out of harm.

Only Patrick was a rotten diplomat. The shul exhausted him, making him blind to the little wars at Headquarters, the schemes of rival commissioners. A healthy, vigorous O'Roarke enabled Patrick to step around the different Irish chiefs without any bother. Once the First Dep began to die in his chair, the chiefs weren't so bashful with the yarmulke boy. They bumped him in the halls. They hid his peeing bottle. Patrick paid no mind to them. He gathered his minyans and watched the shul.

It was Guinness that brought him down. He got abominably pissed one afternoon at the Kings of Munster. He challenged four Innisfree lads to a fight after they insulted the river Shannon. Patrick forgot to hand his gun to the barman. The Innisfree lads stripped him of his holster and shot away the fixtures at the Kings of Munster. The shooting couldn't be hushed. Patrick was called to the firearms board at Headquarters. The chiefs who sat on the board accused him of being a drunken sod who couldn't hold on to his gun. They gave him the choice of resigning, or becoming a clerk.

Lieutenant Scanlan nudged Patrick out of his reverie. "St. Patrick, we've arrived. You'd better grab Jerónimo's hand. They don't let infants into a hospital without a father."

Patrick got out of the car, with Jerónimo clinging to

The Education of Patrick Silver

his soccer shirt. The baby had never been to a hospital, and he was mortified. His fist lay deep in Patrick's shirt. The weather had changed. It was drizzling now. Jerónimo went up the steps of St. Vincent's, his gray head under Patrick's arm, so that the six detectives pushing behind them figured they were in the company of middle-aged twins.

Another detective was standing at the top of the stairs. Fatter and uglier than the rest of Isaac's blue-eyed squad, he'd come out of the hospital to greet Patrick Silver. "Go home, you miserable prick."

"Be nice," Patrick said to Brodsky, Isaac's chauffeur and errand boy. "You'll corrupt the lad. He isn't used to cops who swear. He sleeps in a synagogue. He prays with me."

"Then teach him how to pray for your life."

"Brodsky, your wires are crossed. Isaac sent for us. I'm supposed to see Commissioner Ned."

"Silver, that's a shame. Your timing was always lousy. The great O'Roarke died half an hour ago."

Patrick shambled on the stairs, his stockings at the edge. The baby nearly toppled. He hung on to Patrick with both hands, his ears growing wet.

"Died a half hour ago?" Patrick muttered through his teeth. "Then I'll pay my respects to the corpse."

"Not a chance," Brodsky said. "Isaac doesn't need you any more. He told me to lock the doors in your face."

"Brodsky, I can punch out all your doors. Don't rile me. I'm going in to Commissioner Ned."

Brodsky grinned from his superior position on the

67

stairs. "Silver, your protector is in another world. So walk away from here. You won't have your feet for long without old Ned."

Patrick charged up the stairs. He might have bowled into Brodsky, and gotten through the hospital door, but having to lug Jerónimo hindered his attack. The six detectives caught him by the pants and threw him off the stairs. Patrick rolled onto the curb, with Jerónimo across his chest. Scanlan hovered over him. "St. Patrick, don't sit in the rain."

A growl escaped from Patrick. He wouldn't move. Gradually Jerónimo slipped off his chest. The baby was no fool. He could tell wet from dry. He put his earmuffs on. Patrick's growls grew familiar. "Suck Isaac's eggs." Then he rose up with Jerónimo and hobbled towards the shul.

6

Headquarters was in a powerful slumber during the five days it took to bury Commissioner Ned. All activities ceased. Deputy inspectors wore black ribbons on their coats. The Irish chiefs went uptown to sit with old Ned's coffin. The PC stayed behind his door and wouldn't deliver any mandates. Nothing could happen while O'Roarke was above ground.

Pimloe had a difficult time. He couldn't ascend to O'Roarke's chair before the burial was over. Old Ned began to roll in his box. The corpse pointed a finger at Cowboy Rosenblatt, Pimloe's greatest ally. The First Deputy's office was the one corner of Headquarters that didn't fall asleep; O'Roarke's undercover units had gathered information that Cowboy was accepting bribes from a chain of Brooklyn restaurants. Somebody leaked the news. The PC had to act. He suspended his Chief of Detectives.

Cowboy screamed in his rooms. "Isaac fucked me. He's the guy. I swear to God, I never stole a dime." His rage brought him little bits of nothing. He no longer had three thousand detectives under his command. The Irish chiefs shunned Cowboy's office. They recited Hail Marys around his door. They couldn't think of old Ned without crossing themselves. They were having chills in the first week of August. Their mouths turned gray. They were convinced that Commissioner Ned had the Holy Ghost on his side. How else could a dead man indict a Chief of Detectives?

There was no investiture for Herbert Pimloe. The commissioners couldn't anoint a cop who had been promoted by a thief like Cowboy Rosenblatt. Pimloe seemed loathsome to them now. But the commissioners were beginning to panic. Headquarters couldn't function without a First Dep. They scratched for a candidate. Isaac's was the only face they saw. He was still a tainted man, reckless, obsessed, cursed with a tapeworm and marks on his forehead, so they anointed him halfway. His title was never solemnized. They could drop him in a second. He was made Acting First Deputy Commissioner.

This slight to his integrity didn't bother Isaac the Brave. He had Guzmanns on his mind. But he couldn't chase every celebrant out of his new office. Big and little cops were coming to shake the hand of First Deputy Sidel. The Irish chiefs wished him a long, long tenure (they could be damaged by a First Dep). New-

The Education of Patrick Silver

gate, the FBI man, who worshiped Isaac, envisioned an age of cooperation between his bureau and the high commissioners. It was the FBI man who had huddled with state troopers and agents from Middletown to help Isaac flush the Guzmanns out of Loch Sheldrake. Newgate himself had led the raid on Papa's farm, nearly capturing Jerónimo. Isaac was indebted to him. He allowed the FBI man to move his pillow next to the First Deputy's chair.

Pimloe was the last person to call on Isaac. He'd become a disheveled cop since yesterday, sleeping in his pants. He approached the First Deputy's chair with a miserable face. "Isaac, don't worry. I'm getting out."

Isaac wouldn't let him go. He liked having a Harvard boy scramble for him. "Herbert, I'm making you my number-one whip."

Isaac didn't covet O'Roarke's chair. He had no intention of rampaging through Headquarters. He'd delegate Pimloe to spy on stationhouses and turn marginal thieves into stool pigeons. Isaac was sick of police affairs. The Bronx had cured him of conventional ambition. He agreed to wear a badge with the gold points of a commissioner because it was an excellent blind. The First Deputy could eat up Papa's candy store. Isaac couldn't laugh, couldn't shit without castor oil, couldn't embrace a woman, until the Guzmanns capitulated to him.

A captain of Corrections arrived bringing felicitations from the Inspector General's office. His name was Brummel. He had a small-caliber gun strapped to his chest.

"What happened to Ernesto Parra, the lipstick freak?"

Captain Brummel produced a gigantic loose-leaf book. He went through the pages with a lick of his finger, and brought out a section of the book that was fat as a loaf of bread.

"Brummel, I didn't ask you for a prison encyclopedia. Where's the freak?"

"He hanged himself four months ago," Captain Brummel said, twiddling with the rings of his book.

"And you hide it in a yard of paper."

"Isaac, it was a slip, that's all. A clerk misplaced the file."

"Sure. Brummel, give my regards to the Inspector General and get the fuck out of here."

Isaac wasn't displeased. Ernesto's death supported his case against Jerónimo. The whole of Headquarters could scream at him: Isaac, you're persecuting the baby. Headquarters was wrong. Isaac knew in his bones that Jerónimo was the freak. Little boys died on roofs wherever Papa's baby happened to be. Poor Ernesto was a victim of Cowboy Rosenblatt's lust for solving mysterious crimes. The dollmaker could barely speak a word of English. A team of homicide boys exhorted a confession from him with a series of nods and blinks. Cowboy went on all the local channels with Ernesto's tools, a dollmaker's kit of scarred Exacto knives. These are the murder weapons, Cowboy said. He showed how an Exacto could be used to slice a little boy. Isaac was on Boston Road at the time, working for the Guzmanns, and he couldn't shove him-

The Education of Patrick Silver

self between Cowboy and the dollmaker. Ernesto died in the Tombs.

The Acting First Dep broke away from all his admirers. He walked out of Headquarters with no escorts on his tail. Two battered Chevrolets were waiting for him behind Cortlandt Alley. These weren't ordinary sedans out of a police garage. They belonged to the First Dep's private fleet. They were cars that floated through the City, staying an ugly green all year. Summer or winter, they never got the chance to be indoors.

Isaac was going into the Bronx. He didn't take his chauffeur along. Brodsky had become like an old wife. His presence reminded Isaac of his days as the scourge of Manhattan. The Guzmanns had butchered Isaac's memory. He could only dream of candy stores and white chocolate and Jerónimo's curly head.

A young detective-lieutenant with a blond mustache sat in the front Chevrolet. He had a merciless eye for detail, this Lieutenant Scanlan. He could remember the routes Jorge Guzmann took crossing Boston Road, or what Alejandro wore last Friday, and tell the color of an ice-cream soda from a hundred feet. He was driving for Isaac today.

"Scanlan, roll up your windows. I don't want people getting curious about us."

The Chevrolet was filthy enough to hide Isaac's face. The air turned sour with the windows up. The weather inside the car made Scanlan's eyes swim. The Chevrolet baked to a hundred and twenty degrees. Stuck in a blinding hot storm, Scanlan drove on intuition. "Mother of God," he intoned to himself. Isaac didn't mind a sweating car. He'd always been partial to steam baths.

The two Chevrolets arrived on Boston Road. They didn't tie up with the rest of Isaac's fleet. The First Dep pulled his other sedans off the road. He wouldn't let Scanlan near the candy store. The Chevrolets kept out of sight. Isaac napped with scowls in his head.

He knew Jorge would have to come out of the candy store. Boston Road had once been Papa's exclusive territory. Now his empire shrank to the perimeters of a candy store. He had to send Jorge out twice a day to prove that the Guzmanns were still alive. Jorge couldn't be bullied by detectives in a car. He was Papa's middle child. His fingers behaved like the prongs of a nutcracker when Jorge had you in his grip. He could tear the jaw off a man's head. But Jorge was a sweet Goliath. He wouldn't frighten shopkeepers, babies, and old women. He tickled cats in the Spanish grocery, even if they clawed him. Until you threatened his father's territories, Jorge would never harm you.

Scanlan was too intimidated to poke the First Deputy Commissioner of New York. He leaned over his seat to mutter a few words. "Papa's animal," he said. "Jorge is on the loose." Isaac's scowl disappeared. He woke with a little smile. Isaac had spent six months inside the candy store, smelling Guzmanns while his hair dropped out and a worm grew in his belly. Was it worth giving up his sideburns to see Papa's boys in their underpants? Isaac ate Guzmann chocolate until his face began to rot, but he learned to distinguish among the boys, tell their weaknesses and their peculiar habits. Alejandro played with his prick in bed. Jerónimo could gobble great quantities of white chocolate, but one dark brick would put him in a daze. Topal's thumbs were soft and girlish. Jorge had skinny legs.

The Chevrolets began to move along Boston Road. They followed Jorge for half a block. Papa's boy had a marker in his head. He would drift from lamppost to lamppost, without straying from the curb. Isaac couldn't catch a Guzmann who hugged lampposts. He glowered at Scanlan. "It looks like Jorge's staying on his side of the road."

"He'll cross," Scanlan said, hunched into his seat. "It takes him six lampposts."

Isaac wouldn't reduce Jorge's drifting walk to coordinates of lampposts. He was staring at the bend in Jorge's knees. He'd have to cripple Papa's boy, or the Guzmanns would rat away in their candy store, living on chocolate. Isaac wasn't taking revenge on Jorge's legs. He had to deal in vulnerabilities. Jorge was impenetrable above the waist. His Guzmann chest could defy any number of Chevrolets.

Papa and Zorro were Isaac's enemies, not the boy. He'd played with Jorge in the candy store, building shadows on Papa's wall with a finger, a stocking, and a spool of thread. Jorge could have smashed Isaac's skull, only Jorge was gentle with Isaac, stroking him like a big doll, or a half-brother. Isaac would have preferred to attack Alejandro and Topal, useless boys. But Jorge was the one who could lead him to Papa.

Jorge kept to the line of the curb. Scanlan was

beginning to doubt himself. Should he ask Isaac's permission to climb the sidewalks and run after Jorge? Isaac would have said no. While Scanlan despaired of catching Jorge in the gutters, Jorge stepped off the curb. Scanlan signaled to the second Chevrolet, which cut in front of Jorge. They had him in a sandwich now.

Jorge's mind was closed to fenders and green cars. He thought of the change in his pocket, milky nickels and dimes. He had to buy turnips for his brothers. Papa would fume at Jorge if the bodega man robbed him of a nickel.

Scanlan was on top of the boy. He didn't have time to exult. If he crashed into the other car without Jorge on his bumpers, Isaac would ride him out of Headquarters and drop him into a cow barn for surplus cops. The Chevrolet was choking him. He couldn't breathe in rotten weather. Scanlan had maimed a dog once with this car, never a man. He tried not to look at Jorge's rounded back. He aimed for the rear license plate of the second Chevrolet. Closed windows couldn't protect him from the sound of crumpled bone. It was a terrible noise, much worse than the squeal of metal. Where was Jorge? The two Chevrolets unclapped themselves and crept out of the borough.

Zorro Guzmann, the Fox of Boston Road, stood in a phone booth on Eighth Avenue. He wasn't making telephone calls. This booth was his Manhattan office. Whore merchants would leave notes for him under the telephone box, with descriptions of the girls they wanted: blonde or brunette, with or without beauty marks, with bosoms or lean chests, thirteen or under. The telephone box was free of notes. The whore merchants were going elsewhere for their goods. Zorro had been squeezed out of Port Authority. He couldn't grab runaway girls any more. His talent was still there. He would stroll in a parrot-green shirt and smile into the windows of a bus, with a packet of flowers in his hand. But the terminals were crawling with Isaac's men. Zorro couldn't get near a bus without melting a brown crayon over his cheeks. And no girl would look at a pimp who waxed his face.

It wasn't the death of his business that slapped Zorro under the heart. He stumbled outside the booth. Pedestrians figured a catatonic man was stalking Times Square. Zorro bit his shirt to keep from howling. The attack wouldn't go away. Something had happened to one of his brothers. Nothing smaller than that could have made his chest knock with this sharp a rhythm. The Guzmanns had umbilical cords that could cover the girth of Manhattan island.

The Fox felt paralyzed. His brothers were in two places: the candy store and Silver's shul. Not even the Fox of Boston Road could dash uptown and downtown in a single furious leap. Zorro had to choose. Silver wouldn't let Isaac the Shit hurt Jerónimo, he decided in midstep. So the Fox went north with easterly swipes, bouncing in and out of gypsy cabs. Isaac's blue-eyed detectives had been cautioning Manhattan cabbies about the Fox; he was wanted for sodomizing young girls.

Meddling cabdrivers couldn't alarm Zorro. He would change cabs in the height of traffic, without giving his route away. "Hombre, go straight ahead. I'll show you where to turn." He was the only Guzmann who had graduated from elementary school. But he couldn't go far into the seventh grade. At Herman Ridder Junior High School, on Boston Road, all his teachers pestered him. They filled his brain with irrelevant geography, contradicting his notions of the world, which he got from the candy store.

Zorro knew more about Columbus (Cristóbal Colón) than any of his classmates. Cristóbal was born into a family of Marrano usurers, pickpockets, and thieves. The family fled Spain and went into hiding in Genoa. Around the age of ten Cristóbal became a pimp, then a convict, a murderer, and a religious fanatic. He had a mad conversion in the Genoa prison, believing himself to be the messiah who would lead Marranos, convicts, and the scattered tribes of Israel out of a corrupted Europe. Frightened of Cristóbal Colón's messianic talk, his jailors released him and banned him from Genoa for life.

Cristóbal went to the king of Portugal. The king wasn't interested in convicts and apostate Jews. The monarchs of Spain were more sympathetic to Cristóbal's schemes. He promised them remarkable wealth. He could find the east by sailing due west and award Ferdinand and Isabella with the jewels of India and the island of Cipango (Japan). Seeing a profitable way of getting rid of Jews, they financed Columbus' trip.

Cristóbal was a fraud in Papa's eyes. No Marrano

could ever have thought the world was anything but flat. Falsifying his charts, Columbus sailed east and landed in the Bahamas with his three boats and a crew of convicts and Marrano pimps.

Zorro recited this story to his class at Herman Ridder. The boys and girls tittered behind their desks. "Flat," Zorro insisted. "There aint a bend in Boston Road."

He was called an imbecile, a depraved boy, a hoodlum from a candy store. The brightest girls laughed the hardest at him. "Zorro Guzmann, planets come in spheres." He was gawked at and told to sit down. He stopped going to school.

Zorro had one friend in his class, Manfred Coen, a blue-eyed Boston Road Jew, just Zorro's age. Coen didn't laugh. A flat world was perfectly tolerable to him. Rounded things like balloons and eggs (Coen's dad had a tiny egg store) held no delight for him. Coen and his family spent their summers at Papa's farm. Then Coen decided to draw pictures and attend the High School of Music and Art. He drifted away from Zorro. He became a cop, worked for Isaac the Shit, who tried to exploit the boy's old relationship with the Guzmanns. Trapped between Headquarters and the candy store, Coen died in a crazy duel with one of Zorro's pistols. Zorro couldn't mourn for him. Coen had been fucked by his boss. The big Chief threw Zorro's pistol at Manfred Coen. Isaac was the killer man.

The Fox crayoned his face after sneaking out of the ninth taxicab. He had used up all his brown. His cheeks were Crayola blue. But Zorro didn't have to paint himself for Isaac's fleet of cars. No one was on Boston Road. The Fox stumbled into the candy store, his heart growling at the omen of desolate streets.

The front of the store was deserted. A cop or any other thief could have walked off with Papa's malted machines. Brats could have fingered Papa's jellies and stolen bricks of halvah. The Fox let out a groan. He went into his father's dormitory with his ears dripping blue from crayon sweat. Alejandro and Topal were hiding in their bunk beds under an array of towels, blankets, and sheets, like humps on a mountain. Papa leaned against the wall. He wouldn't give Zorro a recognizable wink, or mutter with his head. Jorge lay on Papa's linoleum floor with bloody pillows over his legs. A team of Marrano witch doctors were with him, men from Uruguay with amulets hanging from their necks, garlic cloves and the fists of dead monkeys.

"Papa, was it Isaac, or the FBI?"

Papa kept to the wall; the ridges along his back told you he was crying, only Papa didn't make a noise. Zorro wouldn't question the witch doctors. He approached his brothers' bunk beds, discovering Alejandro under a sheet.

"Brother, what happened?"

Zorro had listened to Alejandro's muddled talk for thirty-eight years (the Fox would be thirty-nine in October). He didn't falter now. He pulled clusters of words from Alejandro's babble. Devil Isaac. Bumpers. Green cars. The Fox sank down next to Jorge and peeked under the bloody pillows. "Jesus and Moses," he said. He chased the witch doctors out of the candy store.

Zorro, Topal, Alejandro, Jorge, and Jerónimo were *hermanos de padre,* boys without mothers. Papa didn't have any use for a permanent wife. He was an itinerant pimp and pickpocket in Lima, Peru. His boys came from five different wombs. These "aunties," mestizos and marketplace whores, would rear a child for six months and leave. Zorro was the youngest. His "auntie" must have had more brains than the others. He inherited a certain curiosity from her, whoever she was, and the ability to speak in coherent sentences. He was the one child who got restless in the candy store. Even in a flattened world, the Fox had to crawl beyond the limits of Boston Road. And he knew that garlic on a string couldn't heal his brother. Jorge would die unless he was bandaged and given blood.

But Zorro had to shake his father into mobility, and bring Topal and Alejandro out of bed. The Fox didn't hesitate. He wasn't a person who liked to brood over a problem while scratching his balls. He threw the towels off his brothers. "Topal, grab two pillowcases. Pack our winter stuff. We aint coming back. Alejandro, go to the taxi company on Southern Boulevard. Knock on the window, but don't let the hombres drag you inside. They'll steal your shoes. You understand? Knock on the window and make a fist. They'll know we want a limousine. Brother, don't stop for a charlotte russe. We'll be dead before you come home."

The Guzmanns had a chauffeur once, by the name of Boris, but Isaac scared him off the road. Now they had to rely on a portorriqueño limousine service for most of their travel. The Fox and his brothers were city people; none of them could have solved the touch of a steering wheel.

Zorro stroked his father's ear. "Papa, if you don't help me move Jorge, Isaac will finish him and the rest of us. Papa, we can't stay. Isaac murdered the store."

Papa was conscious of the fingers in his ear. Zorro didn't escape him; he knew each of his sons. He was thinking of the Bronx and North America. The Jews here were wild men. Devils like Isaac didn't exist in Peru. Ten months ago Papa had been a citizen of the Bronx, a creature of many properties, with a farm and orchards in Loch Sheldrake, a Westchester graveyard for Marranos only, a numbers bank, and a candy store. He gave money and food to the orphans' asylum, to the Sisters of Charity, to the priests from the Spanish church, to the widows of dead firemen, to gypsies, retarded children, and the poor of Boston Road. The captains of Bronx precincts had drunk malteds with Jerónimo. Detective squads came to Boston Road for Papa's ice cream. The climate changed after Isaac descended upon the candy store, begging for mercy and a job. Detectives wouldn't touch the ice cream. Papa's runners were moody with Isaac in the house. Papa despised his own Peruvian arrogance. He was going to devour Isaac in slow shifts, cannibalize him in the candy store. Isaac was the better cannibal. While Papa ate off small chunks of him, Isaac had started to swallow the candy store, the farm, and Papa's boys.

The Education of Patrick Silver

The fingers were going deeper into Papa's ear.

"Papa, wake up. Jorge's dying in our lap."

Papa left the wall. With a violent energy he stripped all the beds, pieced towels and blankets together with incredible Christian-Jewish knots, and made a stretcher for Jorge. It was an act of desperation and love. The Marranos had spent their lives packing and unpacking, running from home to home. Papa sinned against his children, seeking permanence in the Bronx. America had befuddled him, turned him into a landed baron. Maybe he was wrong about Isaac. Suppose that whore of a cop had been sent by the Lord Adonai to punish Marranos who fattened themselves in America. No matter. Papa could walk away from his fixtures and his malted machines.

It took three Guzmanns to get Jorge into Papa's stretcher of towels, blankets, and rags. They carried him out of the candy store on bended knees. Papa didn't bother locking the store; the vultures would come soon as the Guzmanns disappeared. Grandfathers, pregnant women, and little boys would crawl through the window like a colony of enormous ants and gut the candy store, brutalizing beds, walls, and woodwork; the store would lose its history in half an hour. Bums would sleep in the ravaged dormitory, with newspaper on their heads. Rats would jump out of empty sockets and sniff for crumbs of halvah. The shopkeepers of Boston Road would shrug and say, "Those Guzmann pimps, they ran to Buenos Aires with their millions."

The limousine was waiting for Jorge. Alejandro sat

near the driver, licking a charlotte russe. Zorro didn't begrudge the whipped cream on Alejandro's tongue. How could he reprimand a brother whose memory died every fifteen minutes? The Guzmanns put Jorge on the rear seat. Then Zorro snarled at Miguel, the driver. "Hombre, my brother had a belt, a watch, and cuff links when he came to you. You shouldn't have undressed him without asking permission."

Miguel smiled. "Zorro, you must have left your army somewheres, because all I can see is blood and a pile of shit."

The Fox grabbed Miguel by the wings of his collar. "Hombre, I can buy Mass cards for your funeral without an army."

Miguel opened the glove compartment and fished for Alejandro's goods. "Zorro, I was teasing the boy. Would I steal from a Guzmann? Let the Holy Mother break off my nose if I'm telling a lie. Zorro, where am I taking you?"

"To the orphans' asylum."

"Por Dios, are you committing the whole family? Zorro, they don't accept children over twelve."

The Fox held on to Miguel. "Stop searching. It's not your business to tell me about orphans."

Miguel drove the Guzmanns to Stebbins Avenue. They entered the orphans' asylum through the back, with Jorge on the stretcher. The Fox paid off Miguel. "Hombre, if anybody finds us here, you'll sit with your taxi company at the bottom of the Harlem River. That's for a start. I'll throw your mother, your father, your wife, and your wife's mother out the window. And don't think they'll rest in a grave. I'll tear the bodies out of the ground and hire dogs to piss on them. Hombre, I'll shame you for the next two hundred years."

Miguel walked out with twitching eyes, grateful that he wouldn't have to chauffeur Marranos again. The Guzmanns were having trouble in the asylum. The matrons were furious that a boy was allowed to bleed in their halls. Calvarados, the chief doctor, stepped between his matrons and the Fox. Zorro pinched the doctor's sleeve. "Calvarados, I think we should have a talk."

They went into the doctor's office. Closeted behind a door, without matrons and his brothers, the Fox began to glower. "Calvarados, the Guzmanns have paid your orphans' bills. My father was generous with you. We know a lot about orphans, understand? My family couldn't afford a mother. So we deserve your charity. My brother Jorge will bleed to death if you refuse us."

"Señor, we're not a hospital, we're a children's home."

"I agree. But you're a doctor, and you have a small dispensary, enough to provide for my brother's wounds."

"I beg you, take him to Jacobi, or Bronx-Lebanon. We don't have a blood bank here."

"Calvarados, if I wanted Bronx-Lebanon, would I come to a dump on Stebbins Avenue? Hospitals are cozy with the police, and it's the police who fucked my brother. Don't I have a family outside this door? We'll give you all the blood you need."

"That's impossible," the doctor said. "I can't close off part of the home to accommodate you Guzmanns. The children will get suspicious."

"Calvarados, you aint listening to me. You're the only doctor we can trust. It's a simple thing. My brother's in your hands. So you can't disappoint us. We're terrible mourners. We chew heads in our grief. We start fires. We wouldn't harm an orphan, not me, not my father. But I can't be sure about your staff. Alejandro likes to broil fat ladies. Topal sucks on fingers a lot. Thank God Jerónimo isn't here. He's good for an eyeball and some teeth."

Calvarados surrendered to the Fox.

"Hide us for three days," Zorro said. "Then you're rid of the Guzmanns. Doctor, I swear on Jorge's life, I have a place we can go."

Patrick Silver was in the sanctuary with Jerónimo, Rabbi Hughie, and the elders of the synagogue, saying kaddish for First Deputy O'Roarke. He'd gone to Ned's wake, bringing Jerónimo along, but the Irish undertakers were mean to Jerónimo and wouldn't let Patrick buy indulgences for Ned, or kneel in front of the coffin. Patrick's former brothers, the detectives of the Shillelagh Society, ignored him at the wake, and sneaked off to the nearest Irish bar without inviting him.

So Patrick brought his black ale into the shul and sang the mourner's kaddish, while Jerónimo sulked

The Education of Patrick Silver

under his prayer shawl. The baby had grown quiet since the middle of the week. He no longer mewled. He wouldn't eat dark or light caramels. Patrick would have rushed him to the candy store to see his brothers, only Papa had forbidden Jerónimo to walk on Boston Road.

The baby started mewling towards the end of the kaddish. He wouldn't close his mouth. The prayer shawl whipped around his head. Was he calling Patrick to the window? Silver peeked through a crack in the glass. "God bless," he muttered, seeing a rickety ambulance outside the shul.

Silver removed himself from the prayer box. "Excuse, please." He kissed the tassels on his shawl and went downstairs. The ambulance must have come from a Bronx orphanage. The words STEBB NS AV NUE ORPHAN were painted on its side panel. It drove away, leaving five Guzmanns and a portable hospital bed on the steps of Congregation Limerick. Jorge was under the sheets, with a bluish-white face. When he smiled at Patrick Silver, his cheeks became thin as tissue paper. He had flecks of dried blood in his mouth. His hair was pasted to his skull.

"Irish, are you going to stare at us?" Zorro said. "Jorge had an accident. He ran into Isaac. You get what I mean? Can your church hold a few boarders besides Jerónimo? Irish, they don't like us at the uptown hotels."

Patrick could never get a straight line out of Zorro. The Fox moved and talked in zigzags. "Come in, for Christ's sake. You can have the winter room."

Zorro and his brothers carried the hospital bed over the humps in the outer stairs. Patrick neglected to tell the Fox that the winter room was the unofficial almshouse of Congregation Limerick, a place where beggars could come for a meal and a pillow. But it was the fifteenth of August, and there were no beggars around (they preferred to sleep in doorways until December).

Papa was the last one to enter the shul. The loss of his territories had begun to squeeze him behind the ears. He was wallowing in America. The synagogue frightened him. Papa had never been inside a shul. For five hundred years the Guzmanns of Portugal, Spain, Holland, Lima, and the Bronx avoided God's house, spilling their secret lives into corners and damp rooms. They prayed at home or at the back of the local church, to confuse the *católicos* and humble themselves to the Lord Adonai. Not even a dead Inquisition could push them into a shul. They didn't know how to pray among Jews. They recited the paternoster and asked forgiveness from Adonai.

Jerónimo had gone from the chapel to the winter room to find his father and his brothers. He blinked at Jorge on the hospital bed and began to howl. Patrick, Topal, Alejandro, and Papa couldn't console him. He humped down near the bed and mourned Jorge's blue-white face. Only the Fox could teach him not to cry so loud. "Jerónimo, Jorge will be fine. You and the Irish will feed him soup. But he's not too strong. If you cry, his hair will fall out."

Jerónimo returned to his ordinary mewl. Zorro

hugged his father and his brothers and left the winter room.

"Where's he going?" Patrick said.

"Irish, detectives are looking for me. They could come into your church with their warrants. Why should I give them a second chance at Jorge? It's not smart to have so many Guzmanns under one roof. Irish, watch all my brothers. Adios."

And the Fox ran down the stairs.

PART TWO

7

Odile Leonhardy sat in the Edwardian Room of the Plaza Hotel reading the breakfast menu in a crepe suit without pockets or sleeves. She shared a prestigious balcony table with the film producer Wiatt Stone. The menu wiped her out. The Plaza wouldn't poach an egg for under two dollars. Odile was becoming parsimonious in time for her twentieth birthday. She ate nuts in her room, or depended on Herbert Pimloe to satisfy her lust for French fries.

She'd lived at the Plaza three months, waiting to be discovered by legitimate movie people. She must have picked the wrong hotel. Wiatt was the only producer Odile ever met in the lobby. And the productions he had in mind didn't seem far removed from her old career as Odette the child porno queen. Wiatt fondled her leg under the balcony table and offered her the role

Jerome Charyn

of Abishag, King David's infant nurse, in an epic he was planning on Jerusalem, the City of God. Odile would have to spend the film stroking the loins of a dying king. "I'm too old for that part," she said, using her napkin to pluck Wiatt's hand off her knee.

Wiatt wasn't perturbed. He had Odile wedged in the corner. He could badger her with grapefruits, croissants, and either of his thumbs. "Baby, it's a natural. I want you for *The City of God*. Abishag doesn't stay twelve forever. She ends the film a distinguished lady in King Solomon's bed."

Odile stared at the beamed ceilings of the Edwardian Room, the chandeliers, the pink wallpaper, the exquisite teacups, poached eggs, and the patterns in the chairs, and she made excuses to Wiatt. "Sorry, I have to pee."

She got out of the corner muttering damn! At least with porno moguls like her uncle Vander a girl knew where she stood. Vander didn't snow you with three-dollar grapefruits. He'd squint at a nipple under your crepe de chine and say yes or no. There wouldn't be any talk about Abishag and religious epics. Odile, he'd tell her, I want you to go down on an old king.

She was off the balcony, past a giant strawberry bowl near the reservation table, and out of the Edwardian Room. Men and women in the lobby gulped at her crepe suit. The elevator boy rubbed close to her. Odile had to remind him who she was with a bang of her hip. "Sonny, I'm not your private tree. Lean on somebody else's tit for a change."

She was downstairs with her bags packed before

The Education of Patrick Silver

Wiatt had his second cup of tea. She saw Pimloe come into the hotel. He nearly missed her in her breakfast clothes. She had to wiggle some crepe in front of his eyes. "Herbert, did you just get out of a funeral?"

"Big Isaac put nails in my head. Odile, we'll have to skip the pommes frites for a little while. My stomach's out of commission. Can we meet in the park?"

"Not today. Do me a favor, Herbert. Go into the breakfast room. Ask for Wiatt the film producer. Tell him Abishag's going home."

Odile hadn't stripped herself bare for the Plaza's sake. She kept an apartment on Jane Street. It was a doll's place, a room and a half where she could entertain all sorts of men, cops like Pimloe and customers that Zorro found for her. She was Zorro's girl, but who could rely on the Fox? He would space his visits according to the calendar in his head, sleeping with her on different Mondays of the year. She couldn't understand his preference for Mondays, or the way he could open and close his passion like a fist.

But she wasn't worried about Zorro. The Fox would track her to Jane Street some Monday when his need was great enough. The Guzmanns had their virtues. With Zorro as her protector, Odile was clear of burglars and thieves. Every rat in Manhattan and the Bronx was leery of Zorro and his brothers. If you pimped in their territories, or molested one of their girls, you could lose your neck to brother Jorge.

Odile got to Jane Street in a Checker cab. Being short of cash, she signed her name and the sum of two seventy-five on a slip of paper and gave it to the driver with a hug. He wouldn't carry her luggage up the stairs. So Odile had to make three trips, cursing the incivilities of New York.

The state of her apartment baffled her. There was a saucer on the rug with crumbs in it and banana peels in the sink. Her mirrors were covered with towels. She walked into her tiny bedroom. Zorro was asleep.

"Fox," Odile said, batting the towels off her mirrors. "Fox." She tore at the lavender bedclothes around his feet. He wouldn't wake up. "You crawl into a girl's apartment the second she moves uptown. Guzmann, you're taking advantage of me."

A toe moved. His head turtled out of the sheets. He wouldn't look at Odile. The unclothed mirrors made him gloomy. He muttered something about evil eyes, Peru, and the properties of glass.

Odile was merciful to him. She clothed all her mirrors. "Guzmann, you'd better get out of here. That cop Pimloe likes to follow me. You remember Herbert. Isaac's apprentice. He could be downstairs."

She thought the Fox would jump out of bed. He picked his toenails. "I aint moving for Pimloe. I'll shove him at Isaac with a berry in his mouth."

He told her what happened to Jorge, Papa, and the candy store.

"Zorro, where'd you put your family?"

"In church, with the big Irish."

"You left them with Patrick Silver? God, that dummy came to the Plaza without his shoes."

Zorro was finished yapping with Odile. He caught her by her crepe pants and threw her into the sheets.

The Education of Patrick Silver

He shook off her breakfast clothes as if they were leprous articles. The Fox despised the feel of crepe. Pants on a girl always drove him crazy. He wouldn't allow Odile to hide in any of her decorative husks. He was on his knees licking her body with the salty tongue of the Marranos.

Odile wasn't embarrassed without her clothes. She enjoyed the liberties Zorro took. He wasn't Wiatt Stone with his pinkies under the table. She wouldn't have to be Zorro's Abishag. She'd rather have the Fox in her bed than lie with any old king.

Two days of Zorro, and Odile had wool in her brains. She wasn't a girl who could survive very long without peeking into a mirror. She couldn't wear clothes around the Fox. No panties or ankle bracelets. He wouldn't eat legitimate meals. She had to chew bananas and stay in bed.

The Fox seemed to have a slow recovery. He licked her once and wouldn't go near her again. The Guzmanns behaved like little rabbis. They crept into a girl, writhed, and fell asleep with a pious look on their faces. Odile had gotten down with all six of them at different times of the year. She liked the sound of their orgasms; it was the same melancholy moan. Her other boy friends didn't come like that: loud or soft, their cries couldn't wrench Odile. Only one other boy, a cop named Manfred Coen, had made Odile's teeth chatter against her pillows. And Coen was dead.

She had to get away from the Fox for a little while and breathe air that wasn't perfumed with bananas.

Jerome Charyn

She'd find a mirror in the street, have a good search for wrinkles and moles. It wasn't vanity in Odile; it was the business sense of a girl who was going to sell her face to the movies and had to be aware of every mole.

Odile sneaked out while Zorro was having a snore. She didn't have the patience for underwear. She put on a wraparound skirt and went downstairs. She could have had all the mirrors in the world if she was willing to spy into antique shops on Hudson Street. But Odile was a discouraged girl. She loved Merle Oberon, Mary Astor, and Alice Faye, women of real quality, with generous foreheads and sorrowful eyes, but everybody wanted her to be Odette the porno queen, a spindle with perfect tits.

Going down Jane Street to Abingdon Square she saw Jerónimo and the big Irish standing in the park. The baby mewled at her. "Leohoody." (He liked to call her by her family name.) The Irish wasn't so talkative. He had beautiful gray-white hair. Small black bottles were sticking out of his pants. She adored his great Irish beak. Silver was handsome away from the Plaza.

"What's that in your pockets?" she said.

"Stout."

"Stout?" she said. "What's stout?"

Silver clicked his teeth. He handed her a bottle of Guinness to taste.

"Is it sweet?" she said.

"No. It's black ale."

"Thanks," she said, returning the bottle to Silver's pants. "I don't like bitter drinks."

The Education of Patrick Silver

Silver began to sway in his soccer shirt. "That's a pity," he said. "Because we'll never get on, the two of us. Your not liking Guinness and all. It's got more vitamins than milk."

"Why do you wear that rag of a shirt?"

"Not a rag," he said. "It used to be black and red." He showed her the faded skull and crossbones on the midriff of his shirt. "It's the colors of University College, Cork."

Odile kept frowning at the obscure edges of the crossbones. "Patrick Silver, you're too old for college."

"You didn't get my meaning, miss. It could have been my school, you see, if certain people hadn't chased my father out of Ireland."

She couldn't follow his crazy stories. How do you get from Ireland to Abingdon Square? But she would have liked to discover what was under Patrick's shirt. Did the Irish have gray-white hairs on his chest? She thought of bringing him home to Jane Street, only the Fox was sleeping in her bed. She couldn't undress Patrick at his synagogue. The Guzmanns had overrun the place.

"How's Papa?" she said.

"Alive. He's learning to pray with us."

"Tell him Odile is living on Jane Street again. He can visit whenever he's in the mood. With his boys, or alone. It's all the same to me."

"Any more messages now?"

"Yes. I think there's a cop watching us from both ends of the park."

Jerome Charyn

"I know. The lads belong to Isaac. Not to worry. They eat Baby Ruths and stare a lot. They won't harm you."

Odile kissed Jerónimo and waved to the Irish. If Zorro woke without finding her, he'd bite the walls and swear Odile had abandoned him to the evil eye in her mirrors. She rushed past the blond detective at the top of the park. He smiled at the flimsy opening of her dress, with his cheeks full of candy. "Baby Odile," he said. "Uncle Isaac will give you a whole bunch of presents if you lead him to that stupid Fox."

God, Isaac had his jaws on every block. A dog couldn't piss on a lamppost without some commissioner hearing about it. She ran to Jane Street to warn Zorro about the blond detectives and their Baby Ruths. She came home to an empty bed. The Fox was gone. Maybe he went shopping for bananas. She said shit, shit shit! She could have sunned herself on Abingdon Square and flirted with Jerónimo's Irish keeper.

8

Isaac's "children" moved from Boston Road to Bethune Street. Green Chevrolets were patrolling the Irish synagogue two days after the Guzmanns arrived. Jerónimo could see their wide fins from the different cracks in the chapel windows. Isaac brought his infantry to the steps of the shul. You could find detectives on foot from Washington Street to Abingdon Square. The new First Dep had Silver and all his people in a shoebox. Isaac could suffocate them, or allow them a few inches of peace.

Patrick wouldn't surrender to blue boys and a fleet of Chevrolets. He didn't have to charge into the gutters for random Jews. He could build his minyans inside the shul. Patrick had four new heads to play with: Topal's, Alejandro's, Papa's, and Jorge's. But he wasn't crude. He lured three Guzmanns into the sanctuary, but he wouldn't invade Jorge's bed. He found a yarmulke for Papa's middle child and placed it on the prayer stand after Rabbi Hughie pronounced that a sick person who was already inside the shul didn't have to appear bodily at religious services; he could be represented in spirit and substance by a skullcap or another article of faith, according to the *torah* behind Hughie's ears.

Papa was uneasy in the chapel. Afraid that the Lord Adonai might be offended if an apostate muttered prayers in Hebrew, Papa sang under his breath in Portuguese. He covered himself with a huge linen shawl, just like the elders of the shul. He encouraged Topal not to swing his shoulders until the Torah was removed from the closet near the wall, and he wouldn't let Alejandro crumble halvah on the stairs around the prayer box. But cautioning his sons couldn't relieve Papa's sorrows. How could he forget the Chevrolets? Hearing them gun their motors in the street, he would pull the shawl over his face entirely and withdraw into the only ark a Marrano could make for himself: the dead air in front of his nose.

Seeing Papa in a shroud, Patrick would console him with whispers at the end of a prayer. "Moses, be all right. I don't care a fig if Isaac is king of the sidewalks. He can't climb through windows with a Chevrolet. Be all right."

But he couldn't hold Papa's hand throughout the morning service. Patrick was the guardian of the scrolls. The elders had empowered him to dress and undress the Torah. This, the most sacred office of the

The Education of Patrick Silver

synagogue, was given to Patrick in memory of his father.

There would have been no Congregation Limerick without Murray Silver, the dead vicar of Bethune Street. The wobbly closet that held the scrolls of the synagogue was Murray's ark. It once stood in the King's Island shul of County Limerick. Carved in Baghdad (Patrick learned from his father), the closet went from Iraq to Turkey, from Turkey to Spain, from Spain to Ireland, in the course of seven hundred years. No one dared question the pedigree of the Baghdad closet. It was the holiest vessel in Ireland for the Jews of Wolftone Street. When the mad people of Limerick chased out every Jew, Murray wouldn't permit the ark to rot on King's Island. He carried it to Dublin in a wagon, rowed it across the Irish Sea, and sat with it on a freighter from Liverpool to New York.

Weakened at the corners from its many rides, the closet landed in America with one leg gone. Murray wasn't disturbed. He walked the hobbled ark past immigration officers and moved it into a boardinghouse with the help of a society for penniless Jews. He met a handful of his former congregants at the society, took them to the boardinghouse, where they rejoiced over the survival of the Baghdad closet and made plans for a synagogue that could house Murray's ark.

It was this ancient closet with a tattered Irish curtain over the door (designed by the Jewish weavers of Limerick, the curtain was shedding its hair) that so appalled the Guzmanns. Papa and his boys were convinced that the Lord Adonai lived in the Baghdad closet. They looked for smoke whenever Patrick reached under the curtain. They would shudder as the big Irish brought his Torah to them. The Torah had to be kissed. They would peck at its velvet mantle with crinkled lips. The velvet burnt their mouths. They closed their eyes when Patrick undressed the Torah. They couldn't bear to peek at a raw scroll. The bloodred tongue of Adonai might slap at them from the skein of Hebrew letters.

Except for his periods in the chapel, Papa wouldn't come out of the winter room. He sat with Jorge, winding pieces of string in a mad game of cat's cradle that he would play with himself. Patterns snapped in and out of his fingers at a dizzying rate. Papa had no other occupations.

From time to time Zorro would send doctors into the shul. They were always oldish young men in hospital coats, interns, male nurses, and paramedics that Zorro had bribed away from emergency wards in one of the Little Havanas of the Bronx. Only Zorro's doctors could get Papa off cat's cradle. They would huddle around Jorge, snipping at his bandages with filthy hospital shears, and then have their consultations in a corner of the winter room. This jabber didn't make sense to Papa. They talked of silver kneecaps, spinal fluids, stolen pints of blood. They were eager to turn the main floor of the synagogue into a surgical unit. Masks and little knives began to accumulate near Jorge's bed.

It took Papa a few weeks to discover that these men were poseurs, idiots in hospital coats. They were capable of murdering Jorge with their little knives. He didn't want silver kneecaps on his boy. He threw Zorro's doctors out of the synagogue. They hissed the Fox's name at him from the bottom of the stairs. "The Fox won't like this. The Fox paid us to watch over his brother. Old man, what do you know about medicine?"

Papa wouldn't hold a dialogue with imbeciles. "Tell my youngest that I'm not giving Jorge's knees to you."

Papa called in his Marrano witch doctors. They had much softer faces than the oldish young men. They knew how to cry for a crippled boy. And they were able practitioners. They hovered over the bed, breathing their cloves of garlic into Jorge's wounds. Papa had no difficulty with the cures they mentioned in their chants. They promised manifold resurrections: snow in Jerusalem, restored ankles and knees, hospital beds that could rise up a wall, and the return of all Marranos to Arabic Spain. Papa wept at the news. He was beginning to recover from the stupefaction of a thirty-year roost in the Bronx. America was no country for him. The Marranos couldn't survive around Christians and Jews. But the Spain they were seeking died eight hundred years ago, when the Moors got out of Seville.

Patrick had to feed the Guzmanns and their witch doctors, who were finicky people. Marranos eat with their hands, they announced, scorning Patrick's spoons. They wouldn't touch his sandwiches or his soups. Patrick had to run to a Cuban-Chinese restaurant near the Chelsea Hotel for quantities of pork and black beans.

Jerome Charyn

Attending to the Guzmanns could wear a man out. Patrick escaped to the Kings of Munster whenever there was a lull at the shul. He would snort his Guinness and come back to the winter room utterly smashed, singing bawdy songs (about the witch of Limerick and the traffic under Balls Bridge) that no one understood.

Papa couldn't keep the geography of Ireland in his head. He had his troubles remembering both ends of Bethune Street. Even Boston Road was beginning to disappear. He could forsake a generation of blackberries, malteds, and halvah with the bat of an eye. The chapel was still a frightening place. It had a chair for Elijah and a closet for Adonai. So Papa made his cosmos in the winter room. He could bump into walls with a certain tranquility. He could pester the witch doctors for clearer prophecies. He could wash Jorge's face with a dishtowel. He could observe Patrick's restlessness and hear the groans of his boys. Papa wasn't blind: Topal had a brick in his pocket. What can you do for a boy who stays erect sixteen hours in a row? Papa begged Patrick to bring a prostitute into the house.

"Irish, help me. He's splitting through his pants ... Topal's in danger. His prick could break."

"Moses, I'm sorry for the lad, but you can't have whores in a shul."

"What about Zorro's wife?" Papa said, with a burr in his throat.

"Who's that?"

"The little goya. Odile."

The Education of Patrick Silver

"She can come if she likes," Patrick said. "But not to fornicate. That's the law."

Papa was gritting now. "Didn't know we were visiting in a monastery, Irish. My boys got pricks, thank God. Take them to the little goya, one at a time. Irish, I'm depending on you. Don't lead them into Isaac's fenders. I have one boy without legs. It's enough."

"Moses, not to worry. These are narrow blocks. I can dodge a Chevrolet."

Patrick ran his shuttle from the synagogue to Jane Street. Topal had the greatest need. So he was the first to go with Patrick. "Hold his hand," Papa shouted from the stairs. "Irish, don't let him stumble. He could lose his knees."

They went out of the shul with their hands clapped together. Detectives crowed at them from the green cars. "Patrick, why don't you give this baby to us? We're sweet on Guzmanns. We'll lick his eyes."

"Be gone," Patrick muttered, "before I shit on your windshield," and he dragged Topal away from the cars. He couldn't get into Odile's house. He had to buzz her from the street. "Open up, Miss Leonhardy. I brought a lad for you. Topal Guzmann. And greetings from Papa."

Odile was waiting for him at the door in a party robe. Patrick stood in his black socks. The little goya had patches of skin that could wobble an Irishman's brains. He was becoming a bloody go-between, chauffeuring Guzmann boys to Odile.

"Should I stay in the hall until you've finished with him?"

"No," she said. "Come inside."

He'd been to whores' apartments, but none of them had tea cozies, and waffle irons on the wall. Her bed was tiny. Patrick would have had to cut off his ankles to make himself fit. Papa's little goya was a strange sort of tart. She undressed Topal with affectionate tugs. Was she really married to the Fox? Or did the Guzmanns have a lien on her? Patrick couldn't understand the expansions and contractions of Moses' empire. He was the family strong man, that's all, and caretaker to three of Papa's boys. Topal had a curly chest. His cock flared over his belly, but his scrotum was hard to find. The Guzmanns were precious about their balls. They tucked them away, where no enemy, male or female, could ever dig.

Patrick felt his gums shrink into his head when Odile's robe came off. He couldn't believe the grip her buttocks had on the stems of her thighs. God preserve us, the little goya didn't have a wink of loose flesh. And she wasn't shy around Patrick Silver. She moistened Topal's cock with gobs of spit and climbed on the boy. Patrick withdrew into the kitchen.

He heard a noise like the grunt of a distempered dog. Then nothing. The silence bothered him more than the grunt. A religious man, nearly a vicar at his father's shul, Patrick was no peep. But what could Odile be doing with the boy? He looked out of the kitchen. Topal was sleeping on a pillow (he'd had his pleasure for the month). Odile couldn't have swindled him; there was a deep angelic flush on his face. The little goya sat on the bed without disturbing Topal's sleep. She was in her robe again.

The silk on her legs made Patrick melancholy. He was an Irishman who carried the Torah in his arms. Could he approach the little goya? Offer her some money? She'd say he was included in the Guzmann bill. Hypocrite, he'd lectured to Papa on the sins of fornicating in a shul. He would have hidden Odile in his father's sacred closet and stuck himself to her after prayers. He'd have flung Hughie out the chapel window if the rabbi challenged his rights to the girl. And he'd bite off the face of any elder who interfered with him. Patrick would have his concubine, or he'd close the shul.

The madness of his lust began to frighten him. "Jesus," he said, "I'm going home."

Odile walked into the kitchen. She didn't flirt. She didn't unwind her robe. She didn't put her hand in Silver's pocket. He was dour with her, St. Patrick of the Bethune Street Shul.

"Tell us how you got to be the Fox's bride?"

"Who says I'm a bride?"

"Papa says. Is it a Guzmann fairy tale?"

"No. But it was a rotten wedding. I had to marry six people. Papa and the five boys. It was Zorro's idea."

"That's a good Fox. Was he going to parcel you out like Jerónimo's chocolate? Every Guzmann gets a slice. It's a pity they didn't spread you seven ways, so I could have had my share."

"Don't be crazy," she said. "The Guzmanns weren't interested in a wife. Zorro was collecting marriage certificates. The preacher was a dingbat. He didn't have a church. He had to marry us in the chapel of a Puerto Rican funeral parlor. Zorro figured they couldn't throw Guzmanns out of the country if the whole family married an American girl. I signed the certificates with different names. The preacher didn't care."

"Mrs. Guzmann," Patrick said. "Congratulations."

She pouted at him as she loosened the bindings on her robe. "Don't call me that. A girl can't have six husbands. It's illegal in New York. Besides, I'm underage. I was seventeen when the Guzmanns married me."

Patrick couldn't fight the logic of her arguments, or get to the door. She trapped him in the wings of her robe. The weight of her bosoms on his soccer shirt hit him below the knees. He sank into Odile, numb from the neck down. He wanted nothing more than to hug the little goya, have her nipples in his chest, stand on rubbery stalks, for the rest of his miserable life.

9

There was a history of bachelorhood in Patrick's line. Over the past hundred and fifty years no Silver in Ireland or America had married under the age of forty-five. Murray Silver brought his closet out of Ireland in 1906, as a boy of twenty-two. He labored for his synagogue twenty-five years before he could choose a wife. He was the vicar of Bethune Street, and he despised miserly shuls. Congregation Limerick had to have a proper awning, red and blue glass, and a winter room for the unfortunates who lived around Abingdon Square.

He married Enid Rose, an eighteen-year-old orphan who delivered bread to the shul, in 1931. She was a quietly sensual girl, with hips that broadened out of her many skirts (the vicar met Enid in the winter), and a tongue that could receive a vicar's kiss. Murray was nearing fifty. He had a permanent stoop from climbing up and down the synagogue's ladder to scrub ceilings and replace pieces of stained glass. His Irish brethren throught a young bride would murder him. They advised Murray to take her slow. The vicar said pish! to their advice. He drank black ale and spent himself on Enid.

The elders of the shul were frightened by the signatures of Murray's passion. The girl was pregnant very soon. These old men prayed to God she wouldn't have to carry an orphan in her womb. The elders were wrong about Murray. He survived the birth of Patrick Silver. But Enid caught a cold. It spread to her lungs. She was buried before Patrick could be circumcised.

The boy grew up on the steps of the synagogue. His pabulum came in a dark bottle. He sucked Guinness at the Kings of Munster with his da. While Murray scrubbed ceilings, Patrick slept in the pews with a skullcap over his face. He had his soup in the winter room along with the beggars of Abingdon Square. He lived in the basement with Murray, who gave up his furniture and his apartment after Enid caught her cold. The synagogue was Patrick's new mum. The elders became aunts and uncles to him. And he had the Kings of Munster for a nursery.

Murray began to lose his vigor. He could no longer maintain the synagogue by himself. He would stand on the ladder dreaming of his bride. Patrick had to sweep the shul. He learned to remove splinters from a window, foraging in the cracked glass without cutting his fingers. He prepared a thick soup for surly beggars who

The Education of Patrick Silver

considered it a blow to their dignity that a nine-year-old should feed them. Raised on Guinness, Patrick had the strength to overcome their mean looks. "Kind sirs, it's piss or barley soup," he would say. "Have your pick."

In a few years it didn't matter how often the beggars outnumbered him. At twelve Patrick was a good six feet. He wore a black and red soccer shirt (Murray had swiped the colors of Cork College on his way out of Ireland). The beggars came to respect the skull on Patrick's shirt. If they rioted in the winter room, blowing soup into a neighbor's ear, the boy would pack them in bundles of two and three, roll them down the stairs, and leave them on the sidewalk. He would also protect his father from basement drafts, keeping the vicar in sweaters and double pairs of socks. Murray took to his bed, mumbling Enid, Enid Rose, and falling back into the days of 1931, when he undressed Enid and the Torah with a madman's piety. He lingered for another ten years, dying in 1954, a vicar of seventy.

Now it was Patrick's turn to clutch for a wife. A boy of forty-two, he decided to come out of his bachelorhood sooner than his father did. But his courtship ran into the ground. The girl he wanted to marry was already a bride.

He couldn't go against his employers, the Guzmanns of Manhattan, Lima, and the Bronx, who had their names affixed to Odile's wedding papers. But since he was expected to deliver Jerónimo, Topal, and Alejandro to Jane Street, he had his opportunities with the little goya. He would bring her a yellow rose with disgusting prickles, scarfs from Orchard Street, a charlotte russe, doilies that should have arrived on St. Valentine's Day, chocolates filled with a medicinal sap that Jerónimo himself couldn't swallow.

The Irishman had to be crazy. Odile had never come upon such an assortment of gifts. Although she chided Patrick, stuffing the doilies into his soccer shirt, giving his charlotte russe away, the little goya was pleased. No one else had thought of wooing her in an old-fashioned way. She liked to get down with Patrick Silver on the kitchen floor while one of Papa's babies slept in her bed.

This morning it was Jerónimo. Lying next to Patrick, with her fan puttering in the window, she could hear Jerónimo breathe through his nose. She'd scattered some bedding on the linoleum so Patrick wouldn't scratch his knees. The bedding grew damp in August weather. The gorgeous white hairs on Patrick's chest had the slippery feel of seaweed.

"Irish," she said. "You fuck like Manfred Coen."

Patrick wouldn't talk about a dead cop (Coen had been Isaac's sweetheart, his angel boy). He knew Isaac loved to fish with Coen on the hook, sending his angel into forbidden territories, but Patrick couldn't figure why Coen had to land in Odile's bed. It didn't make him suspicious of Odile. He understood all her avocations, her career with Zorro and other pimps. He intended to marry the whore child. He'd buy her from the Fox if he had to. Patrick wasn't a bloody reformer. He wanted to take Odile off the street. That was it.

The Education of Patrick Silver

There was nothing untoward about the little goya's age. Nineteen? She could grow up in the basement of a synagogue, whoring for one man, Patrick Silver.

His devotion began to frighten her. She'd cling to his chest, satisfy any of his Irish whims, bathe in Guinness if he liked, but she couldn't bear his mumbling about synagogues and brides. The Guzmanns had soured her on the subject of marriage. Patrick wouldn't give up his bride songs. To cool him out, she told him her escapades with Herbert Pimloe, Wiatt Stone (Odile had to lie a little), Zorro, her uncle Vander, and Coen.

Patrick couldn't listen. A series of whimpers came from the bedroom. Jerónimo was waking up. His noises didn't seem like hunger pains. Patrick climbed into his pants. He assumed the baby was lonesome for the synagogue. He peeked in: Jerónimo lay on Odile's bed with his knees in his face. Patrick couldn't understand this tortured position. Jerónimo was shrieking now. Odile called from her swampy bedding. "Did he swallow his fist?"

The baby had his own repertoire of noises. Patrick knew most of it. He could tell when Jerónimo was starving, sick, or sleepy. But the shrieks baffled him until he discovered their melody. Jerónimo was imitating the sound of a fire truck. He had incredible ears. He could isolate a noise from ten blocks away, sing to a fire truck on Houston Street. Patrick only moved when he heard the same shrieks outside the window. He put on his socks faster than Jerónimo could blink his eyes. He didn't kiss Odile, or stick a finger in Jerónimo's scalp. Patrick had no time for minor affections. He muttered, "Esau, stay with me," and ran down the stairs.

The shul was on fire. Smoke spilled from the roofs. The walls crackled. Splits appeared in the stained glass. Patrick shoved into the crowd that collected on Bethune Street to watch a synagogue burn. "Coming through, lads." The two fire trucks parked on Patrick's block were in a comatose state. A single fireman swung close to the shul on an aerial ladder and stabbed at the windows of the sanctuary with a long metal pick. Other firemen kept unwinding enormous bands of hose. The bands went nowhere. They snaked between the firemen's legs and rubbed against the gutters. One of the firemen said something about the water pressure in July.

"The bastard doesn't know what month he's in," Patrick muttered to himself. He couldn't locate a fire chief, but he found the Guzmanns and Rabbi Prince behind the second truck. Jorge was in his hospital bed.

"What happened, for God's sake?"

Papa had a filthy nose. "Irish, who can tell? The fire didn't come from our room. It started in the basement. Another few minutes and Jorge would have had smoke coming out of his ass. Where's the baby?"

"Safe, Moses. He's playing with Odile."

Patrick turned to Rabbi Prince. "Hughie, what did you bring out?"

The Education of Patrick Silver

"Nothing but Jorge Guzmann. And we had a heavy time accomplishing that."

"My father's closet," Patrick said, his eyes getting grim. "Did you leave it in the shul?"

"I've got one pair of shoulders on me, Patrick Silver, and a crooked pair it is. There wasn't enough room on my back for Jorge and the closet."

Why was he behind a fire truck quizzing Moses and Hughie when the closet was inside the shul? Hughie was able to interpret the mad thoughts under Patrick's beetling eyebrows. "Jesus Christ, I'm a rabbi now and then. Wouldn't I have saved the ark if I could?"

But Murray had a stubborn boy. He grabbed an asbestos coat off the back of a fireman. Other firemen yelled at him. "Hey motherfucker, you can't go in." Patrick lifted them out of the way. Wearing the coat over his head like a prayer shawl with skirts and sleeves, he rushed into the shul, closing the door behind him. The heat smacked his nose and made him stagger. Patrick couldn't see a bloody thing. Smoke bellied through the synagogue, hiding the stairs. It ate into Patrick's lungs until his saliva turned a nasty color and he felt a squeeze in his ears. The baking floorboards attacked his dark socks. He had to ride on the nub of his toes. His chest ripped with every swing of his body. He hadn't gone a foot from the door.

Then, flapping the asbestos skirts around his arms, he walked through smoke. Patrick could swear he was losing his skin to the fire. He smelled his own cooked flesh. He'd gotten to the stairs. The bannisters were burning hard. He had to climb with low, hunkering moves, or ignite himself.

Patrick couldn't be far from the sanctuary. He heard the popping of glass. He had to be in the winter room. He sank into mattresses on the floor, his feet snarled in Guzmann blankets and pillowcases. Patrick kicked them off with swipes of his stockings. The saliva became a crust on his lips while he groped for the chapel door. He was in another room. Hughie's study? The shul's brittle toilet? Patrick had his bearings: his knees touched a pew. If he went to the top of the pews and took fifteen paces north, he would miss the prayer box and bang into the closet.

But his calculations failed. He must have run athwart of the closet. He was grounded in the sanctuary, scraping woodwork. The smoke had robbed him of his senses. He searched for his father's leaded windows, that thicket of glass in the north wall. His fireman's coat had begun to crack. The sleeves were ruined. The asbestos near his skull gave off a mean roar. A foul, swollen gas was swimming in the dead air. It flooded Patrick's eyes, nose, and lungs, and the lining of his coat. Bits of his hair were catching fire. He stumbled backwards and forwards, slapping his own head. He saw a tiny flame lick the ends of a gold rag. It was the Irish curtain that hung over the doors of the ark. Hopping like a madman, with his scalp on fire, Patrick found the Baghdad closet.

Outside the shul Rabbi Prince was saying kaddish for Patrick Silver. He hadn't met any flameproof Irishmen in America. There had to be a crazy angel squatting on the chapel wall, in Elijah's chair, an angel who loved to burn down churches and shuls. Which of the angels in the Mishna and the Gemara was a firebug? That one had murdered Patrick Silver.

The Guzmanns stood next to Hughie, mumbling their own prayers. They knew how to mourn for an employee. The Irish was Moses' hired man. He had guarded Jerónimo, befriended Papa's other boys, leading them straight to the little goya, and hid all the Guzmanns (except the Fox) in his shul. Even if Isaac should grab him off the street, Papa would smuggle candles into the Tombs and light them for Patrick. No jail could keep the Guzmanns from paying their respects. They would sing to their fellow prisoners (in English, Spanish, and Portuguese) how Patrick had fared in the war with Isaac the Shit. Papa wouldn't enter the prison mess without screaming Patrick's name. That way the Irish would never be forgotten.

There was a disturbance at the mouth of the shul. The door had swung open. Smoke escaped. The firemen didn't cherish apparitions who danced out of a synagogue. "Crap," they said. "That's a miserable guy." A spook tumbled onto the sidewalk with a closet on his back. He was nothing but a pair of eyes set in a blackened face. He wore a shredded jersey. His stockings were shriveled up. Smoke was coming from his forehead.

The firemen were appalled. They tried to cover him with their asbestos coats. The spook didn't want to be smothered by firemen. His lips parted. He had coaly teeth. His tongue was a disgusting yellow. "Get out of here," he said. "I've got another chore to do."

Five detectives burst into Isaac's sanctuary. Their neckties flew away from their collars. They had buttons off their shirts. Their holsters were awry.

"Mad Patrick is here...."

"He's dressed like a nigger, sir. In black rags."

"We thought he was a Rastafarian. He charges past Security. I almost shot the fuck."

"What's he want from us? He bit Morris on the ass."

"Should we escort mad Patrick to the basement, sir? We could chain him to a filing cabinet and finish him off."

Isaac stared at his five detectives, who made their own little fury in his office. "Be gentle with St. Patrick. I invited him to tea."

There were shivers coming from Isaac's door. You could hear the scratching of knees. Patrick hobbled into the office with two more detectives riding his ankles and his ribs. His famous soccer shirt had lost its sleeves. The crack of his buttocks showed through the top of his pants. His toes curled out of his stockings. He had blood and dark shit on his face, like soot from a fire storm.

"Isaac," he said, with somebody's arm in his mouth. "Are these lads part of your fire patrol? Did they recite a prayer over the kerosine? You shouldn't have touched my shul. If I can get past your fireflies, I'll show you how things were done in Limerick. I'll tear your pizzle off and slap it over your head."

Isaac emerged from the wooden enclaves of his commissioner's desk. "You tin Irishman. The only Limerick you ever saw was your father's pubic hair. You can't fool a tit with your smelly Irish shirt. You were born near Hudson Street, like the rest of us. Only your father diapered you with leftover yarmulkes."

Patrick struggled against the detective who was sitting on his ribs. "Mention my father again, and you'll be living with the worms, Mr. Sidel."

"Let him up," Isaac said. "I'm sick of his blabber. Silver, I'm waiting for you. Push your legs and come to me."

The detectives riding Patrick loosened their hold. He sprang up and seized Isaac by the throat. The two of them started to whirl in the middle of the room. The cops in Isaac's office couldn't believe a common man like Patrick Silver, a refugee from the rubber-gun squad and the janitor of a shul, would dare wrestle with the Acting First Dep. They rushed Patrick Silver, pommeled him, and made grabs at his shirt; pieces of charred cotton came off Patrick Silver and stuck to their fingers. The First Dep shouted at them. "Lay off. Patrick's all mine. I'll fix any mother who interferes with me and him."

So they had to desist. They put their fingers in policeman's handkerchiefs and watched Patrick and the First Dep roll on the floor. They were mystified. They no longer knew how to protect their Chief. They had leather points on their shoes that could penetrate the skull of any Irish giant. But Isaac wouldn't give them the word. All they could do was shut the door and confine the wrestling match to a single room, or the whole of Headquarters would be privy to the news. The story of Isaac groveling with wisps of feathery material in his face would spread to the other offices, arrive at the main hall, and every cop in Manhattan would know that Isaac had wrestled with a janitor.

Isaac wasn't concerned about issues of protocol; he had a thumb in his Adam's apple. He didn't panic, he didn't squeal for help; he was used to ferocious men. He survived six months of standing next to Jorge Guzmann, hadn't he? Isaac had his share of scars; dents in his forehead from a gang of hammer-throwing junkies, a button of flesh on his jaw that was given to him by a crazed thief with a pair of pliers in his hand. Isaac had fought the bandits of all five boroughs and come out alive. He wouldn't succumb to an Irish giant who wore an empty holster like a fucking codpiece.

The detectives couldn't decide what to make of the blood in Isaac's mouth. Was the commissioner choking to death? They were satisfied when they saw Isaac spit out small chunks of enamel. A commissioner couldn't die of a broken tooth. Then Isaac's lot improved. With his sledgehammer elbows he snapped Patrick's chin around and forced the thumb away from his Adam's apple. "Had enough, you stupid son-of-a-bitch?" he said, climbing on top of Patrick.

"I'll stuff turds in your ears before I'm through," the Irishman remarked as he hurled Commissioner Isaac off his chest. It grew into a seesaw affair, with much crossing of elbows and bumping of skulls. Such ambiguous scrabbling gave the detectives fits of insecurity. Nobody would win or lose.

Finally Patrick and Isaac came apart. Both of them lay huffing on the floor. Their faces were grim, their knuckles rubbed blue. Patrick's shirt had disintegrated. He plucked white hairs off his body. Isaac inspected the damage to his mouth. "Bring us some tea," he growled. His staff began to function again. Detectives ran for the commissioner's tea pot, for his favorite honey biscuits, for sugar, spoons, and delicate china. "Now get the fuck out of here."

Alone, without a clutch of nervous hens, Patrick and Isaac drank tea and cognac from blue-veined cups. They didn't speak. They grunted once or twice. Isaac's men stood outside the door and wondered at the periods of silence in the commissioner's room.

The tea had gone to Patrick's head. "Mr. Deputy," he muttered, with cognac blowing off his tongue. "What is it you've got against those Guzmanns? That's a poor clan. You've been skunking Zorro for a year." He slapped the commissioner's desk with the heel of his stocking. "You'd better pick on a different family."

"They murdered Manfred Coen," Isaac said, sniffing the cognac in his teacup.

"Everybody talks about Coen," Patrick said, sucking up more tea while he remembered Odile and that blue-eyed cop of Isaac's. Sad, sweet Manfred was supposed to have been irresistible to the female population of the City. According to the snitches at Headquarters, women couldn't hold up their pants around Blue Eyes

Jerome Charyn

for very long. The Bureau of Special Services loved to steal him from Isaac once or twice a week: Coen was in great demand as a bodyguard for starlets, lady politicians, and the wives of foreign diplomats.

Patrick hugged his knees. There were rumors in Manhattan and the Bronx that Isaac tossed Blue Eyes to the Guzmanns because his daughter, Marilyn the Wild, had gone crazy for Coen. The commissioner had a girl who ran away from all her husbands (she'd been married eight times, Patrick heard) and went to sit on Coen's lap. Patrick used to see her at Headquarters, a daughter that any cop would have been glad to chase if she wasn't so close to their Chief. A skinny, green-eyed girl with tits she was. And an Irish mother (Isaac's estranged wife Kathleen, the real estate goddess, lived in Florida most of the year). The First Dep had no luck with women. His wife, his girlfriends, and his only daughter abandoned him. Marilyn the Wild was in Seattle gathering a new crop of husbands and hiding from her dad.

"Isaac, speak the truth now? Did you sacrifice poor Manfred on account of the lady Marilyn?"

Isaac took a honey biscuit and chewed on it. He'd wrestle Patrick a second time unless the big donkey shut his mouth. "If you're so interested in Coen, why don't you help us trap the Guzmanns?"

"Isaac, that's a pitiful request. What difference can it make to you if the Guzmanns live or die?"

"They put a worm in my gut. I ate their shit for half a year."

"Did you expect Papa to kiss you on both eyebrows?

The Education of Patrick Silver

He knew about your masquerade. Isaac, the fallen Chief. The lad who gave up Manhattan to lie down in a candy store. I was a lousy detective then, the low man on the First Deputy's pole, and even I couldn't believe that Isaac the Pure could ever bring himself to take a bribe from gamblers. You were always so big on logic, making your lovely little charts on the criminal mind like it was a glass ocean you could skate across with your leather shoes."

Patrick's tongue was growing heavy with the froth of his own words, but he wouldn't let Isaac go. "Your logic stinks. You could have had a vacation in the Bronx without your elephant stories. But why did you want to sleep with the Guzmanns in the first place? Is it Papa's hairy legs that turned you on?"

"No," Isaac said, the cognac burning into the hole in his cheek that Silver had made for him. Isaac was mourning his lost tooth. He nearly rose off the carpets from the rawness in his gums.

"Not Papa," he said. "Not Jorge, not Zorro. It's Jerónimo."

Patrick shuddered into his tea. "God damn you, Isaac. Don't revive that ancient story. I'll scream, I'll piss on your walls, if you mention the lipstick freak."

"Jerónimo's a faigele."

"Some faigel," Patrick said. "He does fine with Zorro's wife. Should I tell you how often he's crawled into her bed?"

"You mean the great Odile? I thought she was married to Herbert Pimloe. That girl goes down for an army every night. Name me one man who hasn't fucked Odile."

Patrick didn't give a fig about the commissioner's china. He would have bitten the teacup and presented Isaac with the shards, but he wanted to drive him off the subject of Odile. "Weren't we talking about the baby?"

"Absolutely," Isaac said. "A faigel, I promise you. He likes to mutilate little boys. What can you expect from a family of pimps?"

"You're wrong. Moses didn't raise his boys to attack infants on a roof. I'm the baby's keeper, am I not? Wise to all his habits. I'd know if he went freaking on the roofs."

"He's been stuck at home lately. Ever since the Guzmanns moved in with you. The baby's shy with his father around. But it won't last. The craziness is in his blood. He'll sit on his hands for a while, then he'll have to jump. How long can you live on white chocolate? I give him another week, and he'll be out hunting for boys."

Patrick was tired of cognac in a teacup. He grabbed a corner of Isaac's desk and pulled himself up from the carpets.

"What are you going to do, Isaac? Place a dwarf on every roof?"

"We won't have to. Are you blind? I have enough men on Hudson Street to pick needles off the ground. We'll catch him in the act."

"Isaac, who stuck a fiddle up your ass? Why don't

The Education of Patrick Silver

you push uptown with your lads and burn a few more shuls, you miserable fat shit."

Patrick fled the room, walking on shifty ankles. He was bloated with tea. He passed a maze of offices packed with First Deputy boys. They had malicious smiles for him. "Mad Patrick." These were Isaac's snakes. Patrick could ignore them. He was brooding over more important things. The Chief had called him a tin Irishman, a lad from Bethune Street. I'm as Irish as the toads of Killinane, Patrick should have said. He'd got his Ireland from the neck of a Guinness bottle, studying history and magic at the Kings of Munster, on Murray Silver's knee.

Isaac's men heard him groan to himself. He had an odd look in his eye, this St. Patrick of the Synagogues. His lips were going at an incredible rate. Isaaaac, he said, I knowww about wizards, saints, and kings. Brian Boru, the first king of Munster, he threw the Danes out of Limerick, slapping their heads with a dried bull's pizzle until they dropped their knives and ran down to Skibbereen. St. Briget, abbess of Kildare, she fornicated with the wild fishermen of Dungarvan to keep them from ravaging her community of nuns. The witch of Limerick, a frightful hag, she lived a hundred and ninety years, laying curses on her town, and died of a sneeze that tore her chest. St. Munchin, the hermaphrodite, he brought the lepers into Ireland and suckled them on his own milk. Murray once told him there might have been some Jews among the lepers. How many Silvers drank from Munchin's tit? God knows.

Patrick's thirst for black ale had come from the saints.

Detectives in the halls were squinting at the shreds of clothing on his back. Here's a man that goes in and out of Isaac's den! Who gave him the mumbling lips? They marveled at the powers of their Chief, convincing themselves that the First Dep had turned St. Patrick into a spy. They hadn't noticed Patrick's blue eyes before. "Mother," they said. Isaac had a new "angel," another Manfred Coen.

10

He could have finished the afternoon in his office, had a flunky shave him and pick the remains of Patrick's shirt off his body. The First Dep wasn't a fastidious creature. He could survive with burnt cotton on his face. He had enough tangerines and honey biscuits to outlast the clerks camped around his door. Isaac would sign no documents today. He kept a small apartment on the other side of the Bowery. He could step into his private elevator, walk out of Headquarters, and go to Rivington Street for a bath and a fresh linen suit. But Isaac had lost his bishopric. He wasn't loved on Essex and Delancey any more. He dialed the police garage. "Warm up the Chrysler, will you? And fetch my man. He's probably in the toilet with his comic books."

Now that he was the First Dep, Isaac could avoid the main stairway at Headquarters and bypass other commissioners and other cops. He rode his elevator down to the garage, got into his Chrysler, and shut the door. The air conditioner sucked under his clothes. His thighs were still wet from his match with Patrick Silver. He knocked on the glass partition that isolated him from the driver. "Palisade Avenue," he said. "It's at the end of the Bronx."

Isaac was going to his old apartment up in Riverdale. It belonged to his wife. Kathleen was in Florida converting swamps into condominiums; Isaac could have the apartment to himself. He would find a suit in one of the closets, a silk shirt with brocaded pockets, a hand-painted tie, sets of underwear.

The First Dep ruled over a kingdom of fat and skinny cops; he could turn chief inspectors into patrolmen, flop a whole division, take a man's gun away, groom his own squad of "angels," destroy the Guzmanns one by one, but he was still a slave to Centre Street. He was on call twenty-four hours, like the grubbiest intern at Bellevue. He had an automatic pager on his belt that could summon him back to Headquarters, or put him in touch with the PC. When he got to Riverdale, he would throw the gadget under a pillow and climb into Kathleen's tub.

He didn't feel sorry for the big Irish. St. Patrick shouldn't have dragged the Guzmanns into the shul. Isaac wasn't running a hobby shop at Police Headquarters. He'd smoke the Guzmanns out of all their nests in Manhattan. The First Dep couldn't be accused of starting any fires. Isaac simply told a spy of his (Martin Finch belonged to a gang of pyromaniacs from Cobble

Hill) that he knew of a synagogue that was a perfect firetrap. "Martin, it's ready to fall. A match in the cellar, a whiff of kerosine, and goodbye. But be careful. The janitor's an Irish giant. You'll recognize him by his white hair and his smelly feet. Wait until he goes out for a walk. There's a family of idiots inside. You can burn their noses, but I don't want a funeral pyre. No cremations, you hear? Just get their asses out on the street."

The doormen on Palisade Avenue saluted the First Dep. Isaac had become the celebrity of the house. They'd read articles about him in the *New York Post*, articles that declared Isaac was the brainiest First Dep the City ever had: he lectures at John Jay College, he squeezes criminals, he plays chess.

He found a brassiere and an open pocketbook on Kathleen's parquet floor. Was there a burglar in the house, a crazy guy who liked to sniff brassieres while he went through your belongings? Isaac had a pistol near his gut. But he wasn't going to wag it at a pathetic boy in a duplex apartment. Or search the closets on two floors. He began switching on the lights. A pair of checkered trousers was draped over Kathleen's favorite settee. The boy had a peculiar trademark: he worked in his underpants.

"Come out, you fucker, wherever you are. I'm a cop. Don't make me pull you by your ears."

The burglar jumped out of Kathleen's bedroom, hugging his shirt, tie, sock, and shoes. He was a man of sixty, or sixty-five, with deep gray sideburns and a little belly. Isaac recognized him. He was Miles Falloon, one

Jerome Charyn

of Kathleen's many partners. He plucked his trousers off the settee before Isaac could say hello.

" 'S all right, Miles. Only came for a bath and a change of clothes. Go on back in."

But Falloon had disappeared. Isaac shrugged and started to unbutton his summer jacket. Kathleen watched him from the bedroom door. The real estate goddess was almost fifty-two. The Florida swamps hadn't wrecked her Irish beauty. She was voluptuous in a purple robe. None of the bimbos Isaac knew, girls twenty years younger than his wife, had Kathleen's cleavage. It was like a wound under her throat, a vulnerable patch of skin between her breasts, that could drive Isaac insane after twenty-seven years of marriage.

Isaac was a groom at nineteen, a father at twenty. He'd met the Irish beauty at a real estate office near Echo Park while he was a college student looking for a cheap flat in Washington Heights. Kathleen took her college baby on a real estate tour, making love to him in one empty apartment after the other. Isaac figured he was an amusement for Kathleen, a pastime with a bullish neck, an anonymous boy she kept around during office hours. But she wouldn't let him rent a flat. The college baby had to move in with her. He married Kathleen in a church on Marble Hill, Isaac the skeptical Jew, a Stalinist in 1948, a boy who believed in the forces of history and the erotic truths of his twenty-four-year-old wife.

"Where's your darling?" she said, remaining inside the door.

The Education of Patrick Silver

Would he have to tell her how Ida Stutz threw him over for an accountant with plastic sleeves? Only Kathleen couldn't have heard about Ida in the swamps. The Chief became shrewd with his wife. "I have a lot of darlings," he said. "Which one do you mean?"

"Manfred Coen."

"Blue Eyes? He's dead."

"Then why aren't you wearing a mourner's cloak?"

Isaac began to fumble. "I didn't kill him. It was a stinking family ... the Guzmanns. They had a pistol, Chino Reyes. Manfred slapped him once. The pistol got even. He blew on Manfred with a stolen gun."

"Where were you when it happened, Prince Isaac? You're the holiest cop around. Couldn't you save Manfred Coen?"

"Kathleen, it was an accident. I was only two minutes away."

Kathleen stepped out of the door to scrutinize Isaac. "Turd," she said. "I know your rotten vocabulary. You're always *two minutes away* when you need a good excuse. Now what the hell are you doing here? I didn't call for a chaperone. Who asked you to scare off my friends?"

Isaac gulped the word *Florida*. "I thought you were in the Everglades." He told Kathleen about his desire to crawl into her tub. "I got messed up at work. This crazy Irish Jew tackled me in my office. He would have run home with my neck in his hands if I didn't fight back."

"Look at you," she said. "God bless the Irish Jew.

I'd like to thank him for shoving coal dust in your face."

"It's not coal dust," Isaac said, turning glum. "They're flakes off Patrick Silver's shirt. That lunatic walked out of a fire to wrestle with me."

He could feel some fingers inside his jacket. Kathleen was stripping him. "Get undressed," she growled. "What are you waiting for? Don't you want your bath?"

They went down one flight to Kathleen's master tub, Isaac carrying his gun and soiled clothes. Kathleen stuffed the clothes into her hamper. Isaac climbed over the great wall of the tub. Kathleen had no use for a husband, but she could still admire the firm hold of Isaac's buttocks, the flesh that stood like pliable armor in the middle of his back. She'd stuck with the Jewish bear until her daughter left for college. Then she ran to Florida, and with a realty corporation of nine senior partners (the other eight were all men), she chopped into the Everglades and built a slew of retirement colonies over the swamps. The clerks at her headquarters in Miami were in awe of Kathleen. They had contempt for her partners, whom they considered inferior people. "The lady's got a pair of balls on her," they would murmur to themselves. According to their own calculations, Kathleen was worth a million and a half.

Isaac sat in a puddle of water. Kathleen threw bath oil at his knees. Her breasts looped under the robe. Isaac beckoned her into the tub. "Not a chance," she said. "Prick, I have to be at the airport in an hour. I'm not taking a bath with you."

The bear was getting hungry. His cock rose out of Kathleen's bubblebath. She threw more oil at him. Kathleen wasn't going to fornicate in a sunken bathtub with her own burly husband when she had five millionaires chasing her, Florida men without scars on their body from a murderous hammer, knife, or gun butt.

"Marilyn split with her new man," she said, hurling information at Isaac. His cock fell under the water. His eyes were grim.

"Who told you that?"

"She called me in Miami. I begged her to come down for a visit. I wired her the fare. But she never showed."

"Why didn't she call her father?"

"She's afraid of you. Four husbands in six years. That must be some kind of record. Anyway, it's your fault. She loved Coen. And you kept him from her."

"Coen," Isaac said, splashing with a paw. "I didn't take Blue Eyes out of her bed. But she has a craziness for marriages, that girl. Coen worked for me, remember? I didn't want a son-in-law sitting on my shoulder. Manfred was beautiful, but he had trouble spelling his name. He was an orphan. Orphans don't last. He would have died one way or another."

"But he didn't need a push from you, Prince Isaac."

The Chief couldn't argue with Kathleen. He had a claw in his belly: the worm was migrating again. It grabbed his bowels with a short, hooking rhythm. Isaac had to scream. "Oh my God. Jesus motherfucker shit." The real estate goddess blinked at him.

"Isaac, did you swallow your thumb? What's wrong?"

He slapped around in the water, his knees over his head. He gobbled sounds to Kathleen, who thought her husband was having a fit. He grew pale. His pectorals began to wag. "Worm," he said. "Strangle me. Have to feed the worm."

She didn't laugh at his talk of worms. The bear was whimpering. Then he whistled through his teeth. "Yogurt. Gimme yogurt."

"Isaac, there's no food in the house. I'm only in New York one day a month."

Seeing Isaac grimace, she ran upstairs to her pantry. The shelves were vacant except for a box of tea and an old honey jar. She brought the jar down to Isaac and fed him globs of honey with a spoon. Isaac shivered. The spoon couldn't revive him quick enough. He snatched the jar and ate honey with his tongue. The paleness was gone. Isaac the Brave had sticky cheeks.

"Should I ring the doorman for a chicken bone? I could boil your shoelaces in a cup of tea?"

"It isn't funny," Isaac said. "I caught a tapeworm from the Guzmanns."

"Is it contagious, Isaac? Like the clap? You shouldn't have been so intimate with that family."

"Intimate? Those cocksuckers poisoned me."

Isaac hunkered down in the tub until his lips touched water. Even the most powerful cop in the City

The Education of Patrick Silver

had to soak his balls. The Chief was coming apart. His people had fallen away from him. His father deserted the Sidels when Isaac was eighteen. His mother had been beaten up by a gang of teenage lunatics. She lay in a coma for seven months and died in her sleep while Isaac was in the Bronx with Papa Guzmann. His daughter was in Seattle. Marilyn the Wild ran around the country collecting husbands and discarding them. His angel Manfred was dead because of him. Isaac dropped Coen into his war with the Guzmanns and couldn't get him out in time to preserve the angel's neck. His benefactor, Ned O'Roarke, sat in the First Deputy's chair with a tumor in his throat, and presided over his own death for six years. And his wife Kathleen preferred her share of Florida to Isaac's company.

The tapeworm interested Kathleen. She liked the idea of a tiny animal tugging at Isaac's gut. His suffering began to excite her. He was less of a holy cop with his mouth twisting into a scream. She took off her robe and stepped into the tub with Isaac. The Chief made a powerful snort. It was the old days for Isaac: the college boy waiting to suckle his Irish beauty. He couldn't outgrow his early lusts. He would have been willing to die with his face in Kathleen's chest.

Both of them hopped in the water as they heard a row of disgustingly loud bleats. Kathleen tried to shake the noise out of her ears. "I'm deaf, by God," she squealed. Isaac had to climb around her legs and root for his clothes. He found the automatic pager under a towel on Kathleen's commode. He clicked off the screaming, idiotic thing and apologized to his wife. "Sorry. Can't be helped. That's how my men keep in touch with me."

He dialed his office from the phone in Kathleen's dressing room. Pimloe took the call. "Isaac, the Guzmanns are off the street again."

"Are they living in a gutted synagogue?"

"No."

"Herbert, don't get elliptical with me. Where's Papa and his boys?"

"They moved into a bar."

"What bar?"

"The Kings of Munster. On Horatio Street."

"Herbert, how do you think they got there?"

"I dunno. Is Papa fond of Irish whiskey?"

"Schmuck, St. Patrick sneaked them in. That's his bar. He grew up on Horatio Street. He'll feed Papa Guinness for a while."

"Should we burn them out?"

"Herbert, shut your face. I'll attend to Papa."

"Isaac, don't worry. I have a boy on every roof that connects with the Munster bar. The baby can't walk an inch without our knowing it. Jerónimo's in trouble if we catch him near a roof."

"That's good, Herbert. Goodbye."

Pimloe had become Isaac's dedicated whip. Without Cowboy Rosenblatt, he lost his own ambitions and trapped mosquitoes, gnats, and Guzmanns for Isaac. The Chief went into the bathroom with a smile. He wanted Kathleen and his tub. But the real estate god-

The Education of Patrick Silver

dess was at her vanity table in a blouse and skirt. "Airport," she said. "I'm going now."

Isaac grabbed up his clothes and left Kathleen with Blue Eyes, Marilyn, and Jerónimo bubbling in his fat commissioner's skull.

PART THREE

11

Rabbi Hughie Prince, who read the Talmud with a glazier's strict eye, had declared that any body of land with a roof and four walls could qualify as a synagogue, so long as it housed the holy ark. And Patrick Silver had planted his father's closet in the storage room at the Kings of Munster. Sammy Doyle, the Kings' publican, was shrewd enough to allow the old Jews of Congregation Limerick to pray in his storage room. If Patrick Silver carried his shul into another neighborhood, the Kings of Munster would have to close. Patrick was half of Sammy's trade. The Irish of Abingdon Square showed up at Doyle's bar to drink with the Limerick giant.

Sammy had his problems. The Guzmanns caused him grief. He'd never heard of a shul with five permanent boarders. His customers would talk about the gypsies who lived with him. They blocked traffic into the Kings of Munster. The bar had to accommodate a steady flow of witch doctors (Papa brought them in to change Jorge's bandages and chant over the boy's shattered legs). A stink came out of the sanctuary that clung to the bar for days. Papa was roasting chickens in the storage room. The witch doctors had demanded this offering of chicken flesh to appease the ancient god Baal, protector of the cities, who could heal a crippled boy or wash him into the gutters, depending on his mood.

The publican had to tolerate the stink. He couldn't bother Patrick about it. Silver was in love with the little goya from Jane Street. Sammy had to comfort him when he stumbled into the bar asking for bottles of Guinness. The publican remembered him as a boy. Everybody thought he'd be bigger than the old Munster giant, Cruathair O'Carevaun, who destroyed the harbor at Cork in a fit of rage after he was ordered out of a sailor's brothel somewhere in 1709 (the girls were frightened of what lay under Cruathair's pants). But the Limerick giant stopped growing at twelve. Patrick would stay six-foot-three for the rest of his natural life.

Saying "God bless" with Guinness on his cheek, he moped through the Kings of Munster, which was now a synagogue, a saloon, and a boardinghouse. He left the Kings in his own fit of rage. He was trying to shorten Odile's list of suitors. He would park himself on Jane Street with one of Sammy's brooms (he lost his shillelagh in the fire) and scare away the men who arrived

The Education of Patrick Silver

with flowers and little gifts for Odile. Patrick stood chest to cheek with Pimloe (Herbert was a lot shorter than the Limerick giant) twice a day. Pimloe would dance under Patrick's nose and swear, "I'll crush you, St. Patrick. Do you know who I am? I'm Isaac's new whip. The First Dep can't blink without Herbert Pimloe."

"Then run home to Isaac. Because I'll spank you in the street, Herbert, so help me God."

Patrick was in a fix. He couldn't patrol Jane Street the entire afternoon. He had an appointment uptown. So he left the broom on Odile's steps to remind every caller that his presence was in the house. He plunged east, to the tall hotels and fashionable dormitories of lower Fifth Avenue. He walked up Fifth in his ruined soccer shirt, swabs of cloth trailing from his back like dirty fingers. People crept away from him, children pointing to the man in the shredded shirt who was too poor to wear shoes.

St. Patrick had more than the little goya in his head. His meeting with Isaac puzzled him. A First Dep didn't have to bang shoulders with a retired member of the rubber-gun squad. Did Isaac roll on the ground with him to spit words in Patrick's ear, words about Jerónimo? Passing Thirty-fourth Street, he paused to shout into the window of a men's boutique. "That lad's no faigel. God strike me dead if Jerónimo's the lipstick freak!"

Boys came out of the boutique to stare at the big dummy in rotten clothes. St. Patrick departed from them. He climbed to Fiftieth Street, frowning at the beautiful wallets in a leather store. He preferred simpler goods, wallets that could live with a scratch, shirts that could deteriorate on your body. He was going to visit Odile's uncle, the Broadway angel Vander Child, and discuss Odile's future with him. All his proper clothes, shirts and suits from his detective days, had been destroyed with the Bethune Street shul. He wouldn't borrow a jacket from Hughie. He was Patrick of the Synagogues, apostle of the rough.

Vander's doorman smirked at him. Patrick removed a bottle of Guinness from his pants and nudged the cap off with his teeth. He finished the bottle in one long gulp. "You can tell the squire that his nephew Patrick is coming up."

The doorman rang Vander and told him about the giant in the hall. "A mean one, sir. Claims he's a nephew of yours. He swallowed black piss and left his bottle on the floor." Vander met St. Patrick near the elevator car, shook his hand, and guided him into the apartment.

Patrick drew his shoulders in. He saw room after room of bone-white furniture, highboys that reached over his forehead, lowboys that were broader than three of him. He turned to uncle Vander and made his plea. But the black ale, the walk uptown, and distress over Jerónimo had impaired his speech. Sentences collected under his tongue and broke from him in great mealy blusters. "... marriage certificate ... Zorro ... false wedding ... wife...."

Vander smiled. He'd heard about St. Patrick from his niece. The big dope was plaguing her. He stood outside Odile's building and chased off customers and friends with a broom. No one could get near Odile except Papa Guzmann's idiot boys and St. Patrick himself. His devotion was ruining Odile. She couldn't entertain in her apartment, or undress for a man. She'd become a pauper on account of him.

"Odile doesn't want you on Jane Street, Mr. Silver. You're interfering too much. She's fond of you, I think, but she isn't looking for a grandfather. So keep away."

Patrick got his tongue back. He seized Vander by his lapels, lifted him up so he could be eyeball to eyeball with him, and said, "I'm nobody's grandpa, Mr. Child. I'm a lad of forty-two. My father was a vicar, my mother delivered bread, and I'm going to marry your niece."

He returned to the Kings of Munster, stood the bar to a round of Guinness, blew his nose, and announced his engagement to the little goya. Her many husbands, Papa, Jorge, Alejandro, Topal, and Jerónimo, welcomed Patrick's news. "Irish, I can't speak for Zorro," Papa said. "But you can have my share of her. The goya is yours."

To celebrate, Sammy shoved frozen hamburgers into his automatic oven. "Everybody eats, by God." Papa stared at this sweating box with absolute scorn. He switched the oven off and threw all the hamburgers away. Then he whispered a shopping list into Topal's ear. Topal brought some crayons out of the back room, colored his cheeks to disguise himself, and went to the sausage factory on Hudson Street with his father's list.

While the Irishmen at the bar had another round of
Guinness, Papa made a casserole of sausages and
beans. The aroma of spiced pork baking in a dish
nearly crippled the Irishmen, who had chewed nothing
but flimsy sandwiches and potato chips at the Kings of
Munster.

As keeper of the house Sammy had the right to walk
ahead of his customers and dig into the casserole with a
large spoon. His sampling of the sausages and beans
convinced him that the Kings of Munster shouldn't let
its boarders go. The Irishmen found napkins and plates
in the narrow pantry behind the bar and helped themselves to Papa's casserole. They sat near the Limerick
giant sucking up sausages and beans.

Patrick wouldn't touch the casserole. He sat on a
stool watching Jerónimo play with the Guzmann crayon box. Jerónimo was in the sanctuary. Crouched under the doors of the Babylon closet, he softened crayons with the heat of his thumb. Then he took the
crayons over to Jorge's bed. The baby began to paint
his brother's lips. Jorge smiled with wax on his mouth.
The baby was much more deliberate. His face grew
taut as he applied the wax. He had a keen artistry,
Papa's oldest boy. He moved from Jorge's lips to his
earlobes and his eyes. There was nothing circumstantial about his work. He could account for the irregularities of a cheekbone or an eyebrow. He drew perfect
halos.

Patrick turned away from spying on the two brothers. He had an ugly revelation: Jerónimo was the
lipstick freak. He painted little boys and murdered

The Education of Patrick Silver

them. Patrick had always been a lousy detective. Isaac was the wizard, not Patrick Silver of the rubber-gun squad. The Chief could examine any crime scene and weave a history from a book of matches, blood on a corpse's shoe, movie stubs, phlegm in a handkerchief. But Patrick saw the halos around Jorge's eyes. He could piece together a history from the flight of a crayon in Jerónimo's steady fist. The baby's lines were strong. His elbow never dipped. He judged you with his crayons. He marked you up and took your life away. Jerónimo was the freak.

Did it start with a game? Jerónimo required a docile creature to exercise his art. One of his brothers, or a dollfaced boy. Up to the roofs, hand in hand. The boy must have liked the wax at first. Then he wouldn't sit still. Is that what angered Jerónimo? Made him carve the crayoned boy?

Patrick searched for the weapon Jerónimo used. He found only blunt instruments among the family treasure: ice-cream scoops, plastic whistles, shoelaces made of bone. Where was Jerónimo's knife? Patrick had to crawl into the sanctuary while the Guzmanns were occupied, and Jorge was asleep. He probed every possible hiding place. He wedged his knuckles into the cracks behind the ark and had a miserable time getting them free. He came up with wads of dust and a dead mouse.

Patrick stopped marching to Odile's. He stayed inside the Kings of Munster. He supped black ale with his eyes on Jerónimo and attended to the business of the shul. Rabbi Hughie had placed a collection box on the bar to help the shul entice a cantor for the high holidays. With St. Patrick around, the Irishmen had to reach into their trousers and stuff Hughie's box with dollar bills. Hughie despaired, even with a fat collection box: what cantor would sing the Kol Nidre at the back of a saloon? The shul would have to hire a renegade, a hazan who had been barred from the synagogues of New York.

Patrick couldn't hold the subject of cantors in his head. He was waiting for Jerónimo to jump into the street. The baby wouldn't move. He had his crayon box, his brothers, white chocolate, halvah, and his father's casseroles. Stuck in an Irish bar with nothing to do, Papa took up Sammy's invitation to become the Kings' principal cook. The bar fell heir to a glut of food. Papa didn't limit himself to sausages in a blackbean grave. He had his witch doctors bring Marrano powders and spices to Horatio Street. He prepared dishes that no Irishman had ever dreamed of. Hacked chicken and squid in mounds of yellow rice, garnished with pimentos, olives, and sea cucumber; scallops sliced so thin, they shriveled against your tongue; sauces that could make you sneeze; strips of abalone that curled in your mouth like baby fish; and ten varieties of pork.

Papa's dishes began to pull in Irishmen from other bars. You couldn't find an empty stool at the Kings of Munster from four P.M. to midnight, which were Papa's serving hours. Patrick had to forage through the bar with both elbows out to get his bearings, or the baby would have been lost in the haze of Irishmen. When the crowds became intolerable, he would seek

The Education of Patrick Silver

out the crayon box, knowing that Jerónimo couldn't disappear without his crayons. While the Irishmen gobbled abalone and squid, he would catch the baby staring at him, Jerónimo with a crayon in his mouth, his eyes growing enormous, his ears swelling in the heat, and Patrick having to squint or look down at his stockings.

One afternoon Patrick was waylaid by a dozen Irishmen who obliged him to Indian-wrestle with them all. Patrick took these Irishmen four at a time. With the last of them leaning against his elbow, he happened to twist his face towards the sanctuary. He blinked at the Guzmann territories in the back room, beds, bundles, and floor space. The crayon box wasn't there. "Mercy," Patrick said, flinging Irishmen off his arm. The baby had sneaked out under Patrick's long Irish nose. "Whhere's thaaat childdd?" Sammy's customers flew to the ends of the bar when they heard St. Patrick roar.

Patrick shoved Guinness bottles into his rotting pants, snapped his thighs, and landed on the street. Where would a baby prowl? The old horse barns and factories of Greenwich Street couldn't do Jerónimo any good. The baby would go down to Perry or Charles, Patrick reasoned. Abingdon Square was too crammed with people and cars to pluck a boy off the sidewalk. Patrick went to the top of Charles Street. There wasn't a boy around. Perry Street was filled with touring parties of gay lads who scoffed at a ragged, shoeless, white-haired giant.

Patrick hiked to Bethune Street. Half a block from the scorched shul, he saw Jerónimo walking with a little runt of a boy. The giant followed them on shaky knees. He could find nothing untoward about their walk (Jerónimo didn't paw the runt, grab at the little boy's clothes). He prayed to hairy Esau, unfortunate son of Isaac and Rebekah, to uncloud an Irishman's brain. The runt bothered him. He wore a cap in the summer, a pile coat, and one of his ankles was fatter than the other. Patrick had lived around "fat ankles" for fifteen years; they were a common sight at Police Headquarters. Either the runt suffered from elephantiasis, or he had a holster near his shoe.

Patrick cursed his own gullibility. The runt was a decoy, sent by Isaac to trap Jerónimo and tease him onto the roofs. Patrick had been hasty to judge Jerónimo. Why couldn't Papa's boy walk on Bethune Street? Was it wrong to visit a dead shul? The runt had been put there to seduce Jerónimo. They'd go up to a roof that Isaac had selected in advance. The runt would suck Jerónimo's cheek, according to a special plan. Then the cops would pounce on the baby, handcuff him, and yell freak, freak!

But it couldn't happen if St. Patrick fucked over Isaac the Brave. He tried to warn Jerónimo. Cupping his hands, he shouted into the street. "Jerónimo-o-o-o!" Jerónimo wasn't headed for the roofs. The runt went into the shul with him. "Jesus," Patrick said.

He ran for the shul, the Guinness bottles clinking in his pants. Woozy with beer, the giant had to hold his knees to prevent himself from crashing into the ground. City marshals had thrown up boards around the entrance of the shul. Jerónimo and the runt must have crept under these boards. Patrick couldn't get in. He ripped his fingers clutching wood. He stepped on long carpenter's nails, the rust eating into his heel. He invoked the Munster giant, Cruathair O'Carevaun, to give him strength over the boards. Finally he made a hole big enough to crawl through.

The shul was black as a potato bin. Patrick couldn't see his nose. He kept to a single spot until his eyes grew accustomed to the dark. There were no stairs to climb. The shul stood like a shaved box. The walls still smelled of fire. St. Patrick trudged through pieces of rubble. "Jerónim-o-o-o!" The rubble began to slide. Somebody said "fuck" and "shit." It sounded like a girl. Patrick trudged some more. Flicks of coaly brown light came through the leading in the wall where the stained glass used to be. Jerónimo and the runt were rolling next to Patrick's feet. The runt was a tiny policewoman with cropped hair.

"Miserable spy," Patrick said. He picked her off Jerónimo. She struggled in Patrick's arms, screaming at him with shul dust on her jaw while Jerónimo escaped. She must have lost her handgun in the fracas, because her ankle holster was free.

"You big son-of-a-bitch," she said. "Obstructing a police officer. You'll sit in Riker's Island for that."

Patrick dropped her into the rubble. "A lovely bit of entrapment. Kissing a mad boy in my shul. Pray I don't report you to Isaac."

The lady cop sneered at him. "He tried to kill me, you Irish ape."

"With what? His crayons? Or the pebble in his pants?"

"With this," she said, thrusting a shiny thing into Patrick's hand. It was warm against his skin. Patrick squinted in the potato-bin light and recognized the handle of an ice-cream scoop. The giant pricked himself. The toy was sharp at both ends. Jerónimo must have rubbed it against the pipes in Papa's candy store. Patrick felt a crayon between his toes. He retrieved the crayon box and hobbled out of the shul.

12

A squad of blue-eyed detectives burst into the Kings of Munster with shotguns and a warrant for Jerónimo's arrest (the runt must have told every commissioner at Headquarters how she wrestled with the lipstick freak in St. Patrick's synagogue). The detectives shoved Irishmen aside, stuck their fingers in Papa's casserole, searched behind the bar, leered at Jorge Guzmann, peeked into the Babylon closet, bowed to St. Patrick, and left.

Papa wouldn't serve food that had been touched by Isaac's "angels." He dumped all his abalone and squid into Sammy's garbage pail and started to prepare another casserole. He stirred saffron into a pot of rice and seethed at Patrick Silver.

"You're my man, aint you, Irish? Why did you let them piss on us?"

"Moses, it wasn't the shotguns that bothered me. I know plenty of incantations that would cure a buckshot wound. But you can't fight a judge's signature."

"True, but you can swallow the paper it's written on."

"Moses, what's the good? They'd only come again. Where's Jerónimo?"

"God knows. He's running from you and the cops. Did you have to scare him, Irish? He trusted you."

"Faith, I pulled a runty female off his back. What more could I do?"

"You could have taken his hand and brought him to his father. Zorro had you figured right. He said you and Isaac could snarl for ten years and you'd still end up with your thumb in his ass. Isaac owns your guts. Irish, you're a cop without a badge."

"Zorro's full of crap," St. Patrick said. He dropped Jerónimo's "knife" on the bar. "Moses, there's a toy could scratch anybody's face. Not the sort of plaything you'd expect from a forty-four-year-old lad."

Papa eyed the sharpened stump of metal on Sammy's counter. "Irish, is that your only evidence? Your uncle at Headquarters steals a fucking ice-cream scoop from Boston Road, breaks it in half, and plants a piece of it on Jerónimo, so a prick like you can buy his story. Didn't you catch a lady cop with Jerónimo? Isaac trains a little whore to dress like a boy. Jerónimo can read her disguise. She wiggles her ass at him, and they go into the shul that Isaac burned down. Does that make Jerónimo the lipstick freak?"

"I'm not a Yankee lawyer. I can't argue the delicacies of right and wrong. But if Isaac's wonderboys grab the baby's cuffs, he'll be limping for a long time. Isaac knows how to smile at a judge. They'll build a hole for the baby, and you'll never find him."

Papa touched his lip.

"Moses, I can help you if I get to the baby first. Is he in Manhattan, or the Bronx? Tell me."

Papa shrugged and went to his casserole.

Patrick drifted into the street. The Guinness had begun to boil in his pants. He opened a bottle with his thumb and drank the hot black ale. He got to Abingdon Square with the sun in his eyes. A patrolman in a summer blouse mistook him for a hobo, and dug a billy club into his left wing. "Go on, you scag. Move your shit to the Bowery. Respectable people live around here."

Patrick didn't complain; he allowed the energy in a cop's stick to push him uptown. He'd have to scrape two boroughs for Jerónimo's hideaway. The giant was lost. Should he cover the playground on Little West Twelfth Street? Drudge towards Ninth Avenue? Infiltrate the brownstones of Chelsea? His crooked hops carried him to Twenty-third Street. He had no more bottles in his pants. He'd have to duck into an Irish bar and reload himself with Guinness. Should he get off the streets and follow the baby from roof to roof? While he maundered in the gutters, a dusty cab nearly chopped off his knees. The rear door opened. A familiar grunt beckoned to him from the dark interiors of the cab. "Irish, move your ass."

Patrick ruffled the shaggy ends of his sleeves and

plunged into the cushions. The cab shot away from the cluttered sidewalks of Twenty-third Street. The giant was sitting with Zorro Guzmann, the Fox of Boston Road.

"Congratulations, Irish."

"Zorro, the Guzmanns don't congratulate without a touch of malice. Where did I offend you now?"

"Irish I promise you, it's heartfelt. Papa says you're in love with Odile."

"Papa says a lot of things."

"Take the goya, Irish. Don't cry. Zorro is giving her to you."

"Maybe the goya's not yours to give."

"Why throw insults?" Zorro said, lounging on the cushions. "I own forty percent of her, at least. But who's stingy? Irish, you took care of my brother. That's worth forty percent of any goya."

"Your father thinks I sold the baby to Isaac."

"Don't misjudge him, Irish. He'd murder half the Bronx for Jerónimo." Zorro took the baby's metal toy out of his pocket. "You shouldn't have showed this to Papa. You hurt his feelings."

"Pity," St. Patrick said. "Papa swears it's Isaac's tool, a sinker to drown the baby."

"No," Zorro said. "It belongs to Jerónimo. It stays in his shirt most of the time."

The giant leaned closer to Papa's youngest boy. "Then your father ought to admit who it was that's been tearing up infants on the roofs."

"Irish, you work for us. Remember that. Your job is to protect Jerónimo, not to handcuff him."

The Education of Patrick Silver

"Jesus," Patrick muttered. "What am I supposed to do about the dead little boys? Did you want me to find new bait for Jerónimo? Should I escort him up to the roofs, Señor Zorro?"

"Irish, we aren't like the norteamericanos. You have Zorro's word. My brother won't go near the roofs again."

"I'm grateful for that," St. Patrick said, watching the swollen, heavy streets from his window. Like his forebear, O'Carevaun the giant, he was in the mood to destroy certain property. If Cruathair could dismantle the harbor at Cork, Patrick would chew up Manhattan, block by block, digesting people, lampposts, dogs, and bricks. He had an ungodly rawness in his throat. Patrick's thirst was killing him. "I'm parched," he said, rising out of the cushions. "I'll vomit blood in half a minute. Stop the car."

Zorro had to restrain the giant. "Irish, don't move. We're getting out."

The cab dropped them on Columbus Avenue, in the West Eighties. Zorro tapped the window, and the cab flew downtown. Patrick couldn't remember seeing the driver's face. Could the Fox run a whole fleet of cabs with the twitch of his hand? They went into a Cuban bar on Eighty-ninth Street. Zorro must have known the men in the bar. He rubbed up against these cubanos, saying "hombre, hombre." The cubanos smiled at him with their gold teeth. But they were suspicious of a giant with a holster in his pants. Patrick could feel this angry mugger of eyes surrounding him. He plopped onto a stool, figuring he would have to drink pale beer with the cubanos. "Cerveza de perro," Zorro croaked to the barman.

Patrick's forehead crumpled at the sight of Guinness on the counter. "Mercy," he said. The barman had produced two lovely bottles of black ale. St. Patrick took the miracle without a complaint. "God bless." The bottles were chilled. He warmed them over with his fist (the "fevered" bottles would restore the bitterness that Patrick loved). Then he drank with the Fox.

"Zorro, who turned these lads onto Guinness?"

The Fox had brown foam on his lip. "Irish, you're a pathetic man. Living in a synagogue makes you stupid. How can you see the world with a shawl over your head? There was Guinness in Cuba before an hombre like you could get himself born. The habaneros call it dog's beer. Fathers give it to their young boys. It puts fur on your chest. Irish, let's go. I have to find my brother."

Patrick plagued him with questions once they arrived on the street.

"Is Jerónimo in the neighborhood? Are the cubanos hiding him?"

"Irish, shut up. Coen had an uncle named Sheb. He used to play with Jerónimo. They pissed in the toilet together, they sucked hard-boiled eggs, they took sunbaths outside my father's candy store. Sheb's in an old-age home near Riverside park. That's where we have to look. When my brother gets tired of walking, he'll run to Sheb."

"Coen doesn't die so easy," Patrick said. "Blue Eyes is the tit that everybody uses. Me, you, Isaac, Odile,

The Education of Patrick Silver

Papa, Jerónimo, and this crazy uncle, all of us fed off Coen's milk and blood. Now he won't disappear. You can't pick your feet without finding pieces of Manfred between your toes."

"Hombre, we have work to do. So don't shit in my ear. Isaac isn't an ignorant. He knows my brother's moves. I'll bet he has five cops sitting with Sheb Coen. I can't warn Jerónimo. Isaac's scumbags would kick me into the ground. But you can grab my brother before he gets to the old-age home. Isaac's afraid of your yarmulke and your black socks. He won't mess with a synagogue boy."

A lamppost away from the Cuban bar, and Patrick was hungry for dog's beer again. Mentions of Isaac went straight to his throat. He couldn't even go an Irish mile without lapping on a bottle. Zorro tried to skirt across Broadway. He was worried about the undercover cops who mingled in the crowd of pimps, whores, beggars, cripples, transvestites, widowers, retards, skagheads, snow cone vendors, runaways, pickpockets, and street musicians, and who might recognize the Fox. But the giant squeezed Zorro's shirt and pulled him into an Irish bar, the Claremorris, on Broadway. Patrick was remembered at the Claremorris; he haunted this bar when he was a lad with the First Dep. He could come uptown and drink his Guinness warm, with or without an egg.

"Irish, are you crazy? This is a detectives' bar. You can't walk two inches without breathing on a cop."

"Not to worry," Patrick said. "You're safe with me."

"What about Jerónimo?"

"We'll get to the baby. In a minute. I need some fur on my chest."

Patrick saw a few of his old brothers from the Shillelagh Society. First-grade detectives, they snubbed a cop who had fallen into the life of a janitor and went around in stinky clothes. They assumed Zorro was a rat that Silver had dragged out of his burning shul. Who else would have yellow wax on his cheeks? Patrick didn't give a fig about the frozen attitude of his brothers. He was staring at the holy rump of a girl who danced with four sailors at the back of the Claremorris. Her thighs worked like long, winnowy roots as she plunged from sailor to sailor. Jesus, she had a familiar shape under her narrow skirt. She didn't have to turn her head and wink. That rump belonged to Marilyn the Wild.

What was Isaac's skinny daughter doing in the Claremorris? He couldn't be wrong. He'd spied her often enough as she strolled the corridors at Headquarters on the arm of her husband, who would change from year to year. Patrick disapproved of these husbands. They always had slick leather boots and a tweezed mustache. Every clerk in Isaac's office knew that the girl was in love with Manfred Coen. She would deposit the mustache with her father and hang around Coen's desk. Her father's cops would feast on Marilyn. A blind man couldn't have missed her bosoms, and the draw of her Irish bum. Everybody looked until Isaac came out to glare at Blue Eyes and recall Marilyn the Wild. St. Patrick of the Synagogues, the deacon-detective of Bethune Street, had the stiffest prick in New York City on the days that Marilyn showed.

Patrick would have left her to grind with her sailors, only something was amiss. Marilyn seemed to tire of their company. She had a suitcase under a chair, and the sailors wouldn't allow her to reach for it. The four of them had her in a jumble of arms, legs, and middy blouses. She couldn't break out of the sailors' net. Hands crept up her skirt. The gentlemen at the bar seemed to glorify this multiple courtship of Lady Marilyn. There was much clapping and whistling inside the Claremorris. Such encouragement livened the sailors. Marilyn bounced between their shoulders, her head twisted back, her eyes fixed on the ceiling as four sailors nuzzled her at the same time.

St. Patrick began to pull gentlemen out of his way. "Watch it, lads, coming through."

Zorro hammered on his neck. "Hombre, don't meddle. They love sailors in here. What's that skinny broad to you?"

"She's a friend of mine," Patrick said.

"That's something else. You take their arms, Irish, and I'll go for their balls But make it fast ... what's her name?"

"Marilyn the Wild."

The Fox revealed his teeth. "Hombre, Isaac is out there trying to finish my brother, and you expect me to save his girl? I ought to waltz with those sailors, give them my congratulations."

"Fine," Patrick said. "Then I'll have to bust your

face too. Zorro, don't blame Marilyn for her daddy's shit."

Patrick held two sailors by the nap of their long, square collars and flung them off Lady Marilyn. Zorro grounded a third sailor, biting him just below the knee. The fourth sailor looked up at mad Patrick and rushed out of the bar. The patrons of the Claremorris were furious at Silver and his little toad. They considered it immoral to bite a sailor's knee. The detectives of the Shillelagh Society had tiny blackjacks in their pockets that could cuff the ears of janitors and their friends.

Zorro went into a crouch. He appealed to three of his saints, Moses, Jude, and Simon of the Desert. "Hombre," he whispered, "don't fight with your elbows. We'll never win. Stick your fingers in their eyes."

The Shillelaghs advanced towards Patrick. They liked the idea of a donnybrook in the late afternoon. They were crooning now. They began to leer at Marilyn.

"St. Patrick, do we have permission to dance with your sweetheart?"

"Are you engaged to the bimbo, Pat?"

"Be a good boy. Show us how to bless her quim."

"Hold your tongues," Patrick said. "That's the First Dep's baby. She's Isaac's child."

A stink ran through the Claremorris. The Shillelaghs were smelling their own doom. They'd insulted Father Isaac, said filthy things to Marilyn the Wild. They pitied the loss of their livelihoods. "Lady Marilyn," they said, dusting off her suitcase. "Lady Marilyn."

Patrick took the suitcase from his brothers and

The Education of Patrick Silver

walked Lady Marilyn out of the Claremorris. She hadn't forgotten the sullen Irish giant who shared a desk with Manfred Coen. Her father's cops had dubbed him St. Patrick of the Synagogues because they'd never heard of an Irishman who was so devoted to a shul. Blue Eyes had been fond of the giant. The two of them would sit at their desk eating from a single cup of cottage cheese. Marilyn smiled at St. Patrick. Her ribs were sore from the crush of sailors. She'd stopped at the Claremorris to have a whiskey sour. She felt sorry for one of the sailors and agreed to dance with him (she'd just come home from a sailor's town, Seattle, where lonely boys drifted through the streets dressed in a white that was so absolute, it wouldn't grow dirty in the rain). Marilyn didn't expect dry humps on Broadway; she had to dance with eight knees in her crotch.

"Patrick," she said, "you won't tell my father I'm in Manhattan, will you?"

"Me and your dad aren't much for speaking to one another. Do you need a rooming house? You're welcome to stay with us, if you don't mind sleeping near a whiskey barrel."

"Thanks," she said. "I'll find a place. And I'll visit Isaac when I'm ready for him."

She clutched the suitcase, got on her toes to kiss St. Patrick, then stood level to kiss the Fox, and walked into the thick of Broadway, while the snow cone vendors and other hombres commented on this chica with the fine tits, ass, and legs. The giant would have battled every hombre in the neighborhood to protect Lady

Marilyn (he admired her rump in a more quiet way), but Zorro tugged on his holster.

"Irish, this aint the time. Jerónimo's on the loose."

They had to squeeze between Broadway mamas to get down to Riverside Drive. A green gas boiled up from the sewers. Patrick craved the calm, beery mist inside the Kings of Munster.

Zorro stationed him a block from the Manhattan View Rest Home, where Manfred's uncle lived. Then he disappeared, flicking his tail behind the humped backs of cars parked along Riverside Drive. The giant grew restless waiting for Jerónimo. Images of boys with wounds in their necks entered his skull. The baby had hoodwinked Patrick with those afternoon naps in the old shul. Jerónimo sneaked out of the cellar while Patrick yawned over bottles of ale. With his guardian tucked away at the Kings, Jerónimo could prowl. Patrick rubbed his fists. Mercy, the Guzmanns had used him to shadow the baby's tracks. All the lucre he'd gotten from them, money that kept a shul alive, was smeared with children's guts.

His eyes stayed open. Patrick had sworn himself to Papa Guzmann. He wouldn't betray the clan. He was a lively lookout, standing in his socks; the edges of his shirt twitched in the hot breeze coming off the park. The giant was turning to lead. He didn't want to flag Jerónimo.

How many hours passed? Five? Two? One? It might have snowed in August. Patrick wouldn't move. His white hair had begun to crispen. The rest of him was gray. A stooped boy turned the corner, onto Riverside

The Education of Patrick Silver

Drive. His hair was Patrick's color: white with a shiver of blue. He hugged the walls of apartment buildings, which burnt to a furious orange in the evening sky. The boy galloped through this orange haze. Nothing could interfere with the stab of his knees.

Patrick called to Jerónimo. His forehead thumped with grim reminders of the baby's art: crayons, lips, raw handles, and eyes. God help us all, he couldn't condemn the baby. An Irishman had enough flint in him to set a planet on fire, but he couldn't squeeze affection out of his heart. He put away the monster stories. He was Jerónimo's keeper again. He would steer him off the roofs, hide his crayons and his piece of metal. "Jerónimo."

The baby looked up from the orange bricks. His mouth wriggled open. The skin tightened around his eyes. His stoop deepened. He crept backwards, rocking on his heels, then plunged into Riverside Drive.

"Jerónimo, don't run away from me."

The baby dashed into the gutters. He never got across the street. A car stopped for him. It was Zorro's dusty cab. Patrick could see the Fox through a wormy window. He heard the squeak of a door. The baby's legs were in the air. His belly slid along the cushions; most of him was inside the car.

The giant could have recaptured Jerónimo. He only had to borrow the powers of Cruathair O'Carevaun, hold on to Zorro's bumpers, and hurl the cab into Riverside park. Patrick watched the Fox drive off with Jerónimo. "Brother to brother," he said. "God bless."

He went up to Broadway. He could still have his

dog's beer in an Irish bar. He was the savior of Marilyn the Wild. The Shillelagh Society could announce his many sins: Patrick Silver, the Guzmann slave who lost his gun and fell in love with a Jane Street tart. No matter. He could walk into the Claremorris with his holster sitting like a lame prick on his thigh. None of his old brothers would ever throw him out.

13

The Fox hugged Jerónimo during the ride. It was a greedy embrace. He wanted to feel the knit of his brother's bones, the earmuffs in his pocket, the mothballs every Guzmann crinkled into the cuffs of his shirts (these mothballs could fight the devil's stinky perfume). Zorro wasn't afraid of losing him. Jerónimo wouldn't jump out of the car. The baby looked into Zorro's eyes. He didn't whimper. He didn't flail with his arms. He sat cuddled in Zorro's chest.

The Fox was talking to himself. His eyes were black. He cursed Isaac and Isaac's control over the streets of Manhattan and the Bronx. He knew his father's plans. Moses was leaving America. Zorro could have dodged Isaac's blond angels for the rest of his life, sleeping in telephone booths, eating falafel sandwiches in doorways, pissing into a bottle, waxing his jaws a different color every day of the week, but he couldn't desert his family. Zorro was an American baby. He could thrive in Peru, Mexico, or Isaac's Manhattan. He'd pick your pockets, sell you a girl, take your nickels for a lottery that didn't exist. The Fox enjoyed his nakedness. He could cover himself with wax, mud, newspapers, green stamps. But his father had gathered heavy plumage in the Bronx. And Isaac had plucked him dry. Lost without his farm and his candy store, Moses was sick of the New World.

Zorro could taste his brother's heartbeat. It was strong as Papa's Boston Road curry, spiced with powders that arrived from Uruguay. That was the aroma of the crypto-Jews, hot and sour, the crazy Marranos whose dread and love had the same powerful smell. The Fox's shirt was wet. Was Jerónimo teething against Zorro's stomach? The baby peeked out at the fire escapes on Ninth Avenue. He brooded over ideograms in the windows of fish and poultry stores, smiling when he recognized the snout of a swordfish, chicken feathers, the webbed feet of a duck.

Zorro's taxi probed the truckers' slips behind the markets of Gansevoort Street. The chauffeur, Miguel, was a native of Boston Road. Zorro hired him because the limousine companies of Manhattan were filled with Isaac's spies. Miguel drove for landlords, pimps, and petty thieves like Zorro and Papa Guzmann. He was paid to keep his eyes on the road A chauffeur who got curious about his job might return to the Bronx without any ears. But this skinny borough confused Miguel. He couldn't understand how West Fourth Street could bend far enough to collide with West Thirteenth. Zorro knocked on the glass. Miguel drove into the yard of an old warehouse on Washington Street. He saw a man in the yard: Moses Guzmann.

Miguel tried not to stare. The Guzmanns were touchy people. If your nose wasn't pointed at the ground, Papa thought you were giving him the evil eye. But they had no more instructions for him. The Fox and the baby got out of the car. Miguel hunched into the steering wheel to narrow his line of sight and avoid the Guzmanns' terrible eyebrows, necks, and chins.

Papa wore his cooking smock from the Kings of Munster. He'd escaped from the bar between casseroles and trudged around the corner to Washington Street. Customers would be calling for his squid in half an hour. Papa had little time. He'd left Jorge with Topal and Alejandro. If Isaac's blue-eyed gorillas raided the bar again, Moses would have three missing boys. He manufactured his own weather under the smock. His ribs were cold. He had trembles in his back when he touched the baby.

Zorro whispered in Papa's ear. "We can hide him on the boat."

"Never," Papa said.

"I could go away with him. To Florida. We could live with the cubanos."

"Half the cubanos work for the FBI. They'd sit him in Isaac's lap in two weeks."

"Then let me strangle Isaac, Papa, and we'll have a little rest."

"Another Isaac would come."

Papa watched his youngest boy go slack in the shoulders. The Fox's cheeks were pale under the yellow wax. But his jaws remained grim. Papa had no grand ideas about his family. Four of his boys were idiotas. He'd slept with syphilitic women in the marketplaces of Peru, fornicated like a mongrel dog. None of his wives had a tooth in her head. Zorro was an accident, the only Guzmann whose brains weren't soft. Papa thanked the Lord Adonai every hour of his life for giving him a child who didn't have to count with his thumbs. At an early age Zorro solved the intricate geography of Papa's candy store, and became the Fox of Boston Road. He extended Papa's empire into Manhattan with his natural guile. But he didn't forget his brothers. He adored Topal, Alejandro, Jorge, and Jerónimo, and he looked after them. He showed the boys how to zip their flies. He made an abacus of their fingers, getting them to add and subtract with a furious concentration. He would stall traffic on Boston Road to herd his brothers across the street. Breathing saffron in an Irish bar had clogged Papa's vents: couldn't Moses understand how maddening it was for Zorro to give up one of his brothers? His instinct was to clutch Jerónimo and shit on the world, hold out against Isaac and his Manhattan army.

"César, don't be an ignorant. He won't last a day in the Tombs. The convicts are more vicious than the police. You know the names they'll call him. *Rooster. Queen Jerónimo.* I don't want their ugly hands on his throat."

Papa removed a brick from his cooking shirt; it was

the only weapon he'd carried out of the Bronx. He had himself to blame. He'd seen the mud on Jerónimo's boots. Did it rain in Papa's candy store? The baby fell asleep with wet hair. Papa closed his eyes to the fact that Jerónimo loved to prowl. The baby crawled out the little back window while his brothers were snoring and Papa was fixing ice-cream sodas or deciphering the hieroglyphics of his numbers bank.

Papa's fingers clawed into the brick. He wouldn't let Isaac shove Jerónimo into the Tombs. The baby would never see a jury. The prisioneros at the detention house had their own punishment for molesters and murderers of children. They would choke him to death for playing with the testicles of young boys.

Jerónimo didn't scowl at the brick. He turned his face to Papa. He rubbed Zorro's shoulder with his Guzmann neck. He was thinking of all his brothers. The baby didn't have the word goodbye in his vocabulary. His nostrils sniffed for air. His tongue lay curled on his lip.

The chauffeur, Miguel, prayed to Santa Maria for the courage to hold his chest on the steering wheel and blind himself to the Guzmanns. Miguel was weak. His head peeled over the bottom of the window in time to watch Papa's brick. He would swear on el día de los Inocentes that Papa skulled Jerónimo with a kiss. Either Miguel was crazy, or Papa's elbow didn't move more than an inch. Moses touched Jerónimo between the eyes. The baby crashed into Zorro's arms with a puckered forehead. Miguel slid down into his seat. He would have stayed there for a month unless the

Guzmanns commanded him to rise. The door opened. Miguel heard the scuffle of several bodies. Señora, they had turned his taxi into a hearse!

Someone tapped him on the ear. Miguel wouldn't forget a signal from the Fox. He drove out of the yard. There were two Guzmanns in his mirror. Zorro and the dead baby. Papa wasn't in the car. Jerónimo's brains were mostly blue. He had a swollen head. He sat in Zorro's shoulder, like a live boy. Miguel screamed under his tongue. He was afraid to utter a sound. The Guzmanns could murder you before you had the opportunity to blink.

"Miguel," Zorro said. He wasn't unkind to his chauffeur. He didn't growl. His voice was gentle and low. "Take us uptown."

The chauffeur felt a pinch in his spine. Was the Fox going to caress a dead baby from Fourteenth Street into the Bronx? Miguel was aware that the Guzmanns could provoke a miracle. Any Marrano could make himself into a male witch. Would the Fox breathe into Jerónimo's nose and set the baby to yawn and smile before they got across the Harlem? Would they hold conversations in Miguel's back seat? He squinted into the mirror for obvious signs. He waited for the swelling to go down. If the Fox caressed the baby long enough, the pinkness would return. Jerónimo wouldn't be stuck with blue brains. The Fox was beginning to murmur. Were these the incantations of a Marrano witch, or love songs to a brother? Miguel didn't care. He wanted a resurrection in his car. Who would believe him when he told his compadres that he'd watched a middle-aged boy die and get reborn in under half an hour.

Papa had to cook, or the bar would have grown suspicious. Was there a rat among the Irishmen? Papa couldn't be sure. The brick was under his shirt, hidden from Sammy's customers. The gallants at the Kings of Munster couldn't have noticed Papa's distress. He shredded chunks of abalone with perfect control. His other boys were sleeping in the sanctuary. They would moo for Jerónimo after their heads came off the pillows. What excuse could Papa make? Jorge would bawl with a finger in his eye. Topal and Alejandro would hug behind Silver's holy closet. The bar wouldn't understand their wails.

Moses was sick of breathing Dublin ale. He meant to pack after he prepared his last bowl of squid. The Guzmanns were going to Europe. Now that Spain had a king, young Juan Carlos, the Marranos could return to their original home. Moses would keep out of Madrid. The madrileños were a light-skinned race. Papa would try the north. He would settle in Bardjaluṇa, a city the Arabs helped build. He would live in the old Chinese district, near the oily port, in virtual retirement. He would set up a stall of birdcages on the Ramblas and pick the pockets of Swedish and German tourists. He would take his boys to see Charlie Chaplin films. Zorro wouldn't be content. He would go above the Ramblas, into the boulevards, and drink coffee with pretty girls. He would wear soft scarves and shun Papa's birds. But he wouldn't neglect Jorge and the other two. The Fox adored his brothers.

Silver came into the bar. He looked forlorn. He wouldn't chat with Sammy's customers. He had Guinness in a corner, without a taste of Papa's squid. The giant didn't bother peeking for Jerónimo. He was the only Irishman at the Kings of Munster who understood where the baby was.

The giant wasn't Papa's chattel any more. But he couldn't get free of the Guzmanns. He was tied to that miserable family. He realized the choices Papa had. Once the baby was arrested, even the Marrano saints couldn't have kept him alive. Papa had to hide him, or put him to sleep.

Moses and the Irish were watching one another. They could grieve without opening their mouths. They didn't embrace. Nothing passed between them except the sad energy in the coloring of their eyes. Patrick sucked on a bottle without leaving his corner. Papa attended to the squid.

PART FOUR

14

Each Thursday morning in September a blue limousine would park outside the John Jay College of Criminal Justice to deliver Father Isaac. The Chief had to make his eleven o'clock class. He was lecturing on the sociology of crime. His students were a privileged lot. Patrolmen, firemen, and sanitation boys, they had never sat in a class with the First Deputy Police Commissioner of New York. They were crazy for Isaac. He would talk to them about Aeschylus, with a gun sticking out of his pants. They would go dizzy from his insights, his remembrance of poets, hangmen, crooks, politicians, and carnival freaks.

The First Dep had one liability: his automatic pager would force him in and out of class. The bleeps coming from the region of his tie could curl the ears off any student. Patrolmen and firemen wagged their heads until Isaac turned off his gadget and got to the telephone in the hall.

On this Thursday morning Isaac was morose. Headquarters switched him to a gravedigger's shack in Bronxville, New York. He grumbled to Herbert Pimloe, who picked up the phone. "I'm lecturing, Herbert. What's so important?"

"We found the baby," Pimloe said.

Isaac felt a crack in his mouth. "Where, Herbert?"

"In the Guzmann yard. Isaac, you were right. The fucks buried him in the family plot. I swear to God. It took an hour to dig him up. Isaac, you couldn't believe the bones in that yard. Papa must be an orderly guy. He sank all his enemies in the same place. You remember that creepy runner of his, little Isidoro? I think he's down there, sleeping with Jerónimo. We sent for the morgue wagon. Isaac, should we wait for you?"

"No," Isaac said, his mind drifting to the vultures at the morgue who would hover over Jerónimo, pathologists from Bellevue with their dissecting kits, tubes, laboratory handguns, airtight jars for liver and kidney samples.

"Herbert, call Bellevue. Tell them to cancel the truck."

Pimloe stood in the gravedigger's shack with the phone stuck in his cheek, waiting for the First Dep to clarify himself. Father Isaac didn't mutter a word. "Why should I stop the truck?" Pimloe finally said.

"Because we're leaving the baby in the ground."

The Chief was deranged. The PC would come down

on them all if he discovered that Jerónimo hadn't been exhumed. Pimloe had to supervise a team of gravediggers to get at Jerónimo. They'd been pushing bones around since a quarter to seven.

"Isaac, the baby has a dent in his skull. That's Guzmann work, if you ask me. What about Isidoro? Isaac, look how many corpses we could pin on the tribe. The Fox can't squeeze out of this."

"Herbert, button up the mess you made and go home to your wife."

Father Isaac returned to his section of firemen and cops. There was a wormy boy in his head. He didn't feel like jabbering about Aeschylus, blood, and crime. His pager began to scream again. Isaac dismissed the class.

He didn't have to argue with Herbert Pimloe. Headquarters switched him to another location. He had his old chauffeur on the wire, Sergeant Brodsky, calling from a West Street diner. Brodsky was jubilant. "Isaac, the Guzmanns belong to us. They're booked on a Spanish freighter. Barcelona's the last stop. Isaac, imagine. They used your name. They registered as the four Sidels. What fucking nerve they have. They're on board this minute. They carried Jorge in a mattress. Isaac, I didn't see Jerónimo."

"Jerónimo's on top of the Bronx," Isaac said.

Brodsky scratched his nose. "What d'you mean?"

"The baby isn't going to Barcelona."

"Isaac, have a heart. Is the moron with you, or Pimloe? You want me to raid the boat? We got sledgehammers. I could chop that pier to shit and pull Zorro off his Spanish freighter."

"Brodsky, the Guzmanns can do whatever they please. Zorro doesn't exist for us. Let Papa have his ocean voyage. The Atlantic will be good for Jorge's legs."

"God, Isaac, can't I collar one of them? Just one? Alejandro, or Topal. I don't care."

"Brodsky, goodbye."

Isaac got to Horatio Street in his blue limousine. He dismissed his driver with a polite nod and entered the Kings of Munster. Irishmen fled from the bar. The lone dog in the place, an ancient terrier who loved to lick empty Guinness bottles, scampered under a table. Sammy wouldn't say hello. Isaac ground his teeth and walked into the sanctuary. Patrick had his minyan. He didn't need Father Isaac. He was standing with Rabbi Hughie and the elders of the shul, and three bearded gentlemen in soft white prayer shawls. "Cover your head," Patrick growled. "You're in a holy room."

Isaac put a handkerchief over his ears.

"Silver, I didn't mean for the baby to die."

"Isaac, don't bring your rotten business into my father's house. This is a synagogue. We pray here. We don't mention the police."

The three bearded men began to wail in their soft white shawls. The shawls obscured parts of their anatomy. Either they had humps on their backs, or they were leaning too hard. They collected near the Babylon closet without a prayer book among them.

The Education of Patrick Silver

Isaac whispered now. "Who are they? Greenwich Avenue mystics?"

Patrick glowered at Father Isaac.

"Papa sent them to us. They're cantors from Peru. Isaac, close your mouth. The cantors are singing Kol Nidre for the shul."

Isaac had to whisper again. "Forgive me, Silver. I'm not a rabbi. I'm a cop. But who sings Kol Nidre ten days before Yom Kippur?"

"The cantors have a different calendar, Isaac. Leave them alone. They celebrate Yom Kippur whenever they can."

Isaac listened to the Peruvian cantors. Their singing made no sense. Was it a muddle of Spagnuolo and Portuguese? Only the Marranos could recite the Kol Nidre in a variety of tongues. It didn't matter to Isaac. The rhythm these cantors could produce, the warbling sounds that seemed to shatter inside their throats, appealed to Isaac's worm. His belly turned smooth. The flesh under his heart didn't have any claws. But the handkerchief was quiet on his skull. The First Dep wouldn't sway to the cantors' melody. They screamed with enormous tears in their eyes. Isaac hardened himself. He knew about the reputation of Marrano cantors and priests. The best of them had the power to stir the dead. Isaac didn't want to hear Jerónimo chirp at him from a Westchester grave. He left the Kings of Munster.

People saw a man with a hankie over his ears. Isaac couldn't outrun the cantors' wails. Their Kol Nidre stuck to his body like a cloak of thick, wet fur that was making him stink. He couldn't go back to Headquarters. He'd have to watch the furniture men dismantle his desk and move all the drawers to Chatham Square. Isaac was the last commissioner to remain on Centre Street. The Irish chieftains were already installed in their brick fortress next to Chinatown. After this month Isaac would be chewing green tea with his fellow commissioners in the mandarin restaurants of Bayard Street.

He crossed the Bowery with crooked eyebrows. The worm was beginning to crawl. He couldn't take a step without squeezing his belly. Someone barked at him from the window of a Ludlow Street restaurant. It was his old "fiancée," Ida Stutz. She came out of the restaurant to gape at Isaac.

"You expecting a sun shower?" Ida said. "Or is it a cap for your brains?"

Isaac remembered the handkerchief. He took it off.

"Where's your husband?" he said, with a canker in his voice.

Ida blanched. "Who could get married with blintzes on the fire? ... what husband?"

"Your accountant, Luxenberg. The one with plastic on his sleeves."

"That embezzler? Isaac, did you ever see such a man? He hides behind my shoulder so he can monkey with the restaurant's books. Luxenberg wiped us out."

"Why didn't you tell me? I could have ripped the plastic off his arms."

The Education of Patrick Silver

"You were busy with the Guzmanns," Ida said. "Who could talk to a commissioner like you?"

Isaac looked sad without the handkerchief. He was no longer bishop of the lower East Side. Ida began to take on the musk of an old "fiancée." She could have fallen on Isaac in the street, hugged him under his commissioner's jacket.

"Isaac, should I meet you at your place, or mine?"

"Mine," Isaac said.

"Mister, give me twenty minutes. I have a potato pie in the oven."

Isaac went to his flat on Rivington Street. He had two small rooms, where he could shuck off his clothes and get clear of his obligations at Headquarters. At home he was a boy with garters on his legs, not the Acting First Deputy Commissioner of New York. Isaac didn't have to turn his key. The door was unlocked. He wondered if Papa had left a few "cantors" for him, gentlemen from Peru with mallets in their sleeves that could erase Isaac's memory, knock the stuffing off his scalp. Isaac would greet Papa's "cantors" with gruff hellos. He didn't hesitate. He walked inside without fingering his gun.

A naked woman sat in his kitchen tub, smoking a cigarette. How could Isaac mistake the tits of Marilyn the Wild? It wasn't every father who could peek at his daughter's chest. He heard a whistling in his ears. Would the Irish-Jewish fairies who guarded Patrick's shul burn out his eyes for squinting at Lady Marilyn? Isaac must have had a prissy worm in his gut. It grabbed his colon with a spiteful energy that drove his knees together and sent him crashing into the side of the tub.

"Christ," he said, "can't you put something on?"

He gave her a shirt to wear. Marilyn got out of the tub with a sinuous move that startled Isaac. He wouldn't stare at the wall while Marilyn pushed her body into his shirt. The shirt came down to the soft furrows at the front of her knees. A clothed Marilyn couldn't help Isaac the Brave. The proximity of his girl—the bittersweet aroma rising off her hair, the curve of her neck against one of his own collars, the penguinlike awkwardness of her kneecaps—unedged the Chief. He wished he could arrive at his fiftieth birthday without a daughter. He couldn't exist in a single room with Marilyn the Wild.

"I won't bother you for long," she said. "I didn't want to live in a crummy hotel until I found an apartment. I'll be out of here in a week."

"Fuck an apartment," Isaac said. "You can stay with me. It's not as stupid as you think. Marilyn, I'm never here."

"You wouldn't like the friends I brought upstairs."

"Bring whoever you want."

"What about Blue Eyes?" she said.

Isaac cursed all his fathers who had given him a daughter that could bite. His tongue was trapped in his mouth. The Chief had to sputter. "Marilyn, not my fault. I got enemies. Manfred happened to grow up with them. It was a shitty piece of work. I had to bounce him at the Guzmanns . . . I had no choice."

"Balls," she said. "Manfred would be alive today if he went with me to Seattle. I tried to steal him from the police. He wouldn't budge. He was devoted to a prick like you."

"Seattle," Isaac said, his cheeks a horrible color. "Blue Eyes couldn't have made it in Seattle. It's too wet. The rain would have warped his Ping-Pong balls. He'd have had to come back to us."

"Papa, why is it that everybody around you dies, and you walk away without a scratch on your ass."

"Not true," Isaac said. "I have plenty of scratches if you care to look."

The Chief stumbled in his own room, searching for his honey jar. Marilyn had depleted him. Isaac had to have his lick of honey, or die. Marilyn caught him with his finger in a jar. Isaac, the sorry bear.

"Papa, should I run down for a dozen eggs?"

The bear was whimpering with honey on his nose. Daughter, I've got a worm that's more precious to me than all my battle scars. Didn't I catch it in the field? It's with me when I shit, when I snore, when I go to John Jay. It can spell "Blue Eyes" with the hooks in its mouth. A goddamn educated worm.

The mad, Peruvian Kol Nidre wailed in Isaac's head. He was surrounded by priests. Whose design was it? Big fat cop, Isaac the Brave, murdered Blue Eyes, murdered Jerónimo, how many more had he managed to kill? He didn't need a gun. He snuffed you out with logistics. Isaac was lord of Manhattan and the Bronx. He worked you into a corner, and let someone else supply the instruments. You couldn't shove your pinkie into his face. Isaac was always clean. He loved that blue-eyed bitch. Hadn't he nourished Coen for ten years? Marilyn should have picked a high commissioner for her man, not a cop who played checkers with Isaac. He didn't want Coen to fuck his daughter. It rankled Isaac. Blue Eyes was a piece of him. Should he have spent his life imagining his own "angel" rutting with Marilyn the Wild?

There was a knock on Isaac's door. The Chief recalled his date with the blintze queen. Now he'd have a surplus of women in his room. Marilyn and Ida would stalk one another and growl at Father Isaac. "Baby," he said, touching Marilyn on her long, long sleeve. "It's only a friend. Ida Stutz."

15

St. Patrick of the Synagogues courted the little goya with Jerónimo in his brain. He stood outside her building with his new shillelagh, discouraging suitors, girlfriends, and pimps. There was a bit of pishogue in his snarl, a touch of Irish sadness in the handle of his broom. Silver had helped destroy the baby. He'd allowed Jerónimo to drift into the war zones that Isaac had manufactured as a kind of plaything, a dollhouse for the Guzmanns and himself. Damn their rotten armies. Patrick was the baby's keeper, and he'd let him slip away.

His pants weighed down with Guinness, his shirt corroding on his chest, Patrick kept to Jane Street, singing about witches and dead Irish kings. It was a freakish serenade. Odile's windows were in the back. All she could hear was a wretched yodeling and a blather of words. She would come downstairs in a gauzy nightgown to collect St. Patrick. Neighbors spied her buttocks under the gauze, lovely moons of flesh, as she got the Irishman and his bottles into her tiny flat. He built up a passion off the street. Odile had shallow bruises on her neck from St. Patrick's grizzled chin. He made love to her in a serious way. The little goya could scarcely breathe, with a giant living on her bed. His climaxes caused the walls to shake. His whole body rumbled during one of his spectacular comes.

After the lovemaking he would suck on his bottles and devour a loaf of bread. Then he lay back, belched, broke wind (his farts had a timbre that could have healed a sick dog), and sang to Odile, mumbled songs that terrified her.

> There was a lad named Jerónimo
> Who caught a disease, a disease
> In his father's candy store.
> He saw Moses giving little boys
> Licorice and ice cream
> Licorice and ice cream
> And he wanted to color their lips
> Color their lips
> With his father's crayons.

"Jesus," Patrick said, "were they going to cure him with a dose of halvah? Why didn't they put the lad in a hospital? Couldn't Papa discourage little boys from visiting the candy store? Who's going to pray for the infants who died on the roofs?"

St. Patrick would weep with bread in his mouth and gorge his throat with Guinness. He discovered a circular on Odile's dressing table, an advertisement for the Nude Miss America Follies. "What's this?"

"Nothing," she said, and she snatched the circular from out of his hands. "They slipped it under the door. Crazy people. Can't stop inventing new contests."

"Is that an entry blank at the bottom of the page?"

"Didn't notice," she said, stuffing the circular into her nightgown. She would shriek if she heard another song about Jerónimo. The goya missed that weird family. The Guzmanns had provided for her, given her customers and pocket money. She'd gotten one postcard from Zorro. He scratched out thirteen words to Odile. "Love it here. You can smell the shit under the streets. Love. César."

Odile was approaching twenty. She'd retired from porno films eleven months ago. Living at the Plaza had thrown her into obscurity. Producers couldn't keep their noses out of her tits. The men she knew wouldn't honor the emotions of a nineteen-year-old. They wanted a mechanical baby, a doll with nipples that could go hard and soft. But Patrick was in the way. That idiot Irishman talked marriage in her ear. He'd make Odile into a washerwoman yet. She'd have to scrub the drawers of every rabbi at the Kings of Munster.

Odile had to break off with the Irishman. She couldn't earn a penny with St. Patrick guarding the house. She packed a suitcase of cosmetics and underpants and ran from Jane Street the next time Patrick attended morning prayers. She picked a good hideout, where she would be safe from any man. It was a lesbian bar on Thirteenth Street called The Dwarf. She could play parcheesi in the back room, eat cucumber salads while she sandpapered her bunions for the Nude Miss America Follies. It wasn't vanity that compelled Odile. She didn't need two thousand men to admire the geometry of her pubic hair. It was business, nothing but business. If she won the Follies, she could revive her stage name, Odette, and become a porno queen again.

The bouncers at The Dwarf were broadshouldered cousins, Sweeney and Janice. The cousins could sniff out transvestites, FBI agents, and undercover cops for miles around The Dwarf. Both of them were in love with Odile. They hadn't seen the little bitch in over a year. Janice wasn't utterly pleased with Odile's invasion of the premises. That girl created havoc at The Dwarf. Bartendresses wouldn't mix drinks. Customers quarreled. Everybody wanted to dance with Odile.

Janice came up to her table. The bitch was wearing a mint julep face masque, light green mud that was supposed to purify her skin.

"Honey, there's a man outside. I think he belongs to you."

The mud splintered close to Odile's eyes. "Shit," she said. "How did that Irishman find this place?" She walked over to the window. She smiled through the mud. It was only Herbert Pimloe. He arrived at The Dwarf in a wilted cotton suit. Isaac's whip forgot his handkerchief. He wiped his forehead with the ends of his tie. The mudpack made him sulky. He was frightened of a girl with green jaws.

"Odile, what the fuck?"

She wouldn't stand on the sidewalk with Pimloe. "Herbert, I'm in training. Go away."

Pimloe had a cowish look. "I want to live with you."

"Herbert, your wife wouldn't appreciate that."

"So what? I'm never home more than twice a week. I swear. Isaac keeps me in Manhattan."

"Are you the big Jew's baby?"

Pimloe jumped in his cotton suit. "Who says?"

"Patrick Silver."

Pimloe began to sneer. "That quiff. He got burned out of his own synagogue. Odile, Isaac can't sign his name without me. I'm a chief inspector now. Silver's a cunt who wears a naked holster on his belly."

"Don't curse," she said. "I might decide to marry him."

Odile retreated into The Dwarf and left Pimloe flat. He intended to hop over the doorsill and chase Odile, but the image of Sweeney and Janice in their tailored suits soured him. The whip returned to Headquarters. He would raid the bar tomorrow with a squad of blue-eyed cops and drag those fat cousins into the street so he could be alone with Odile. Pimloe was a Harvard man. He would convince the girl to stay with him, bribe her with promises of champagne, chocolate, and pommes frites.

The little goya didn't have time to dawdle over

Herbert the cop. She had to peel mud off her face. Sweeney lent her a small valise to hold her nightgown in. Janice wouldn't wish her luck at the Follies, or say goodbye. Sweeney pushed her out the door with a soft kiss. "You don't have to undress for those pig men. You can stick to parcheesi with Janice and me. I'll be at the show. If the pigs try to handle you, I'll tear up the floors."

Odile hiked to the Greenwich Avenue Art Theatre with Sweeney's valise. Posters of nubile ladies and girls had been slapped to the theatre walls. The creatures on the walls existed without a blemish; the girls had amazing white teeth and no brown spots on their nipples. Odile wondered how many photographers had been paid to brush beauty marks off the posters (even the porno queen had a few baby moles on her ass). She went in to register herself.

The manager of the Follies, Martin Light, ogled Odile. He sat in his undershirt distributing pink cards to all the Follies girls. It was sweltering inside the Greenwich. Martin couldn't get the thermostat to dip below ninety degrees. He held onto Odile's wrist for half a minute. "Baby, it's a lousy crop this year. You'll walk away with everything. I can tell." He winked and sent her into the bullpen that had been set up behind the stage for the convenience of the Follies girls.

Odile was grossly uncomfortable around such girls. They giggled, chewed gum, and had scowls under their eyes that betokened a mad determination to walk on stage without their clothes. It saddened Odile. None of

The Education of Patrick Silver

them could compete against the perfect ripple of her bosoms, and the cool outline of her back and legs.

Odile got into her nightgown and stood away from the girls, who prowled in their kimonos, pajamas, and little robes, or rubbed against the walls in bikini underpants. The air grew thick in the bullpen. The ceiling began to cloud with the girls' hot breath. Pajamas came off. Panties were flung across the room. The Follies girls had a passion for getting undressed.

They had a visit from Martin Light. The manager plowed through a bullpen of sweating nipples. He stopped at Odile. This one was in her nightgown. The sight of gauzy material in the midst of so many yards of flesh unsettled Martin. He laid a finger on her hip. "Girlie, you can't lose. Meet me after the show."

Odile did stretches and pliés in her nightgown to prevent her arms and legs from falling asleep. The Follies girls watched this litheness of Odile with swollen faces. They began to despise their own raw bodies. They had lumps on their behinds that couldn't be smoothed away with all the stretching in the world. They might have finished Odile, ripped the gauze off her shoulders, devoured her fingernails, if the manager hadn't come for his girls.

He herded them out of the bullpen, keeping the girls in a scraggly line. They bumped knees wherever they went. You could hear shouts and muttering through the walls of the bullpen. The auditorium was alive. The girls didn't see a thing. Stumbling in the dark, between paper walls, they couldn't determine chairs, aisles, or the shape of individual men.

Martin led the girls into a pit under the stage that was inhabited by a clutch of fiddlers and trumpet players. Amplifiers and trumpet cases were packed near the girls' feet. No one could bend without striking an amplifier. The girls had to lick each other's hair, or learn to breathe in a new way. Martin took his undershirt off. Grinning murderously, he powdered his neck, his bald spot, and his eyes, and slipped a dinner jacket over his bare chest. There were scars in the velvet sleeves. A cuff was missing. Martin held his grin. He squeezed around the girls, fumbling into elbows, hairdos, and pieces of crotch, and climbed out of the pit on tiny, wicked stairs. You could say goodbye to the nudie show if you lost your footing. You would have tumbled into the fiddlers and broken your head.

Martin pranced on stage with his traveling microphone, while Odile brooded in the pit. The fiddlers scraped on their instruments. Spit from the trumpets flew into Odile's eye. The little goya began to sob. She was stuck with the Follies girls, pinned to their bellies and their crinkled behinds. She couldn't run home to The Dwarf.

The girls mounted the Greenwich stairs, smiling, one by one. None of them fell. Martin shouted their names to the audience. "Here she is, lovely Monica, the pride of Kips Bay. A hundred and three pounds in the flesh. Good people, what do you say to Monica?"

Odile had to guess the audience's mind from her station in the pit. She heard a lot of booing for Laura of Washington Heights, Tina of Hudson Street, Monica of Kips Bay. Monica never returned to the pit. Did

Martin hide a girl after the boos and the stamping of feet that could swallow the noise of his fiddlers? The girls in the pit were moaning now. Ushers had to hoist them up the stairs when their names were called (the audience was surly in the lull between the presentation of girls).

"Odile of Jane Street," Martin said. No usher had to drag her out. She grew dizzy on the stairs. She saw the fiddlers' brains. She stepped out of her nightgown and continued to climb. The stage lights turned her body raisin blue. "Also known as Odette," Martin cried into the microphone, his powdered neck deep inside the dinner jacket. No one hissed at him. The audience mooed for Odile. She didn't have to jiggle her parts. The natural sway of her bosoms in the raisin-colored light could stun an auditorium.

There was whimpering in the front row. Handkerchiefs sailed off the balconies. "Oh my God, oh my God, oh my God."

Martin crouched behind Odile. He had her by the ankles. "Girlie, don't leave. The theatre's in love with you."

Odile prayed for her deliverance. It would take a whole contingent of girlfriends from The Dwarf to get her out of the Greenwich Art Theatre. Sweeney didn't come. Odile stayed frozen in the light, with Martin on her ankles. Only Zorro could have saved her. The Fox would have gone from seat to seat slitting men's throats until the auditorium emptied out. But Zorro wasn't in the United States.

The little goya heard a bellowing over the chorus of

moos. There had to be a rhinoceros in the house. "Put on your clothes." She saw a hand grab Martin Light and bowl him across the stage. The hand belonged to Patrick Silver. Men were clinging to his back. The giant shook them off with a twirl of his neck. He had blood in his ears. "Jesus," he said. St. Patrick didn't want to fight an army of lovesick men. He was grieving for Jerónimo.

The giant would recite the mourner's prayers on a little bench at the Kings of Munster. But he couldn't say kaddish all day long. He was lonely for Odile. He prowled the streets with Guinness bottles in his pants. Then he read the marquee at the Greenwich. Nude Miss. His head wasn't right. American Follies. His brains were pissed over with Irish beer. He stumbled into the theatre without buying a ticket. Ushers whacked him with their flashlights while Patrick squinted at the stage. He saw precious ugly women shake their hips under a wrinkle of blue-black light. "It must be market day at Kilkenny." People told him to get quiet.

He crossed his elbows and leaned against the wall, weary of so much shivering flesh, until Martin Light announced Odile. St. Patrick cleared the aisle. He dumped men and boys over the backs of chairs. A rabbit bit him on the ass. Patrick howled. "Jesus, I'm through." Fingernails scraped his nose. His ear was on fire. He reached the pit with entire bodies clamped to his leg. He had to slap down two heads to raise his thigh. He tore into the fiddlers, climbed the treacherous

The Education of Patrick Silver

stairs, dispatched Martin Light, and tunneled into the curtains with Odile.

The auditorium rose up against St. Patrick. Men from the orchestra and the lower balconies jumped onto the stage. They would have murdered the giant to hold on to Odile. They didn't have sturdy weapons. They had to slap him with buckles, fists, and shoes. The shirt came off St. Patrick's back. His trousers fell below his hips and stood clinging to his buttocks. Fists and shoes made squeaky noises on Patrick's skull. The buckles stamped red dents into his shoulder blade. The giant was growing angry.

"Esau," he muttered, "where's your daddy now?"

Cradling Odile in one of his armpits, he began to fight. He pummeled noses and eyes, struck at Greenwich Avenue gentlemen with his elbows, chin, and knees. They were caught in a September whirlwind that none of them could describe. You couldn't get close to Patrick Silver. The storm around him could fling a man over the lip of the stage. Patrick didn't have to grovel in the memory of Brian Boru. The witch of Limerick was only a frizzled hag with all her hundred and ninety years. Patrick could have destroyed the Greenwich Art Theatre with the wind he produced on stage. He couldn't restore Jerónimo, protect the Guzmanns in Barcelona, sing to Manfred Coen, but he could break out of Martin's bullpen with the little goya.

Living in a heated armpit, with Patrick's blood pounding in her face, Odile had gotten used to the giant. She wouldn't let go of his chest.

Patrick shouted into her ear. "Jesus, will you marry me?"

The little goya thought she would die. The whistling in her head attacked the insides of her cheek. But the deafness was only temporary. The whistling went away. She laughed and nibbled his armpit.

16

Moses was a tradesman again. He acquired fourteen parrots. Sleepy birds with bald shoulders and hairlines in their beaks, they were without a particular pedigree. Papa couldn't have told you whether he had macaws, Amazon birds, or cockatoos. The parrots seemed reluctant to move their heavy brains. But Papa could cure them of their sluggishness for a price. If the turistas dropped a few Barcelona pennies on the counter of his stall, Moses would whisper to the birds, prod their bellies with a piece of wire, grin at them, until they showed a bit of liveliness. They would break walnuts with their stunted bills, scoop berries out of Papa's fist, do somersaults inside their cages, sing raucous one-word songs.

These were English birds. They could scream "Piss" at you, or mention Isaac the Brave. The parrots' exotic coats had been given to them by Moses, who painted their feathers every other week. He allowed the birds to dry in the outhouse that belonged to the Guzmann flat on the Calle Reina Amalia, in the Barrio Chino. Topal and Alejandro had to squat down with parrots over their ears.

Zorro snickered at Papa's outhouse. He wasn't going to drop his pants in the vicinity of birds that told you when to piss. The Fox couldn't get Manhattan plumbing out of his head. He would relieve himself in the mirrored toilet at the Hotel Presidente, throwing ten pesetas to the concierge. He always wore an orange suit inside the Presidente; he wouldn't buy any of his furnishings at a men's shop on the Paseo de Gracia. Zorro's handkerchiefs, cuff links, shoelaces, socks, and ties came from Boston Road.

The Fox had his morning chore. He would bring Jorge to Moses' stall on the Ramblas, while his father and brothers carried the birds. Moses and the boys would sit on their bench dreaming of Jerónimo. Absorbed in themselves, they forgot to swipe pocketbooks from the German tourists. They would have starved without Zorro's thumbs. Even the parrots were at his mercy.

It was childish work for the Fox. With an American handkerchief covering half his chest, he walked up and down the Ramblas, brushing against turistas who crowded the stalls. He avoided the pillbox hats of the guardia civil as he moved away from the stalls with a wallet under his handkerchief. Sometimes he took a parrot along. The bird would nest on his shoulder, with its claws in Zorro's summer wool, its beak inside his hair.

Zorro didn't endure birdshit on his clothes for the sake of companionship. The parrot helped him steal. The turistas would marvel at the plumage on a sleepy bird, while Zorro went in and out of their pockets. He could earn nine hundred pesetas in an hour.

The bird dug into his shoulder today. Zorro could smell the paint on its wing. He stopped at the Calle del Hospital for a café tinto and mocha ice cream. The bird woke long enough to peck at Zorro's mocha. "Cocksucker," Zorro said.

The bird sprayed ice cream on the Fox. Zorro would have banged its head into the stones of the Barrio Chino, or slapped its damaged bill, but he had stolen goods in his pocket and he didn't want to bring attention to himself.

The Barcelinos mistook him for a pimp. You couldn't have found another orange suit in all of Catalan (it had been put together by a Polish tailor in the Bronx). Zorro gave up pimping when his brother died. He was barely a thief. He wouldn't have plagued the turistas if his father and the birds were able to feed themselves. He would have strolled under the statue of Columbus in the harbor, lunched on fisherman's soup near the Calle del Paradis. He would have posed for Germans, Italians, and Swedish tourists, with the parrot on his shoulder, and wheedled pesetas out of them. Then he could pee at the Presidente or the Ritz, go to Barcelonita, and sit on the Muelle de Pescadores, at the edge of the city, and throw one of his shoelaces in the Mediterranean. The scum would buoy it up. A shoelace never drowns in Barcelonita.

"Jerónimo."

Zorro turned his cheek. The parrot was nibbling on his brains. He stared into its left eye. The eye was smudged with yellow paint.

"Don't you mention my brother," Zorro said. "I'll tear your neck off, you bald piece of shit."

The Barcelinos stared at man and bird.

Zorro finished his café tinto. The parrot nudged Zorro's ear. He fed it the last of his ice cream. The mocha began to fill the splinters in its beak. Zorro swabbed the bird with his handkerchief. They left the Calle del Hospital and continued down to the sea.

NEW FROM BARD
DISTINGUISHED MODERN FICTION

EMPEROR OF THE AMAZON, Marcio Souza   76240 $2.75
A bawdy epic of a Brazilian adventurer. "Mr. Souza belongs in the same room where a Garcia Marquez, a Jose Donoso, a Vargas Llosa, a Carlos Fuentes and a Julio Cortazar disport themselves....A remarkable debut."   *New York Times*

THE NEW LIFE HOTEL, Edward Hower   76372 $2.95
A novel of discovery and entangled love, set in an African country on the brink of upheaval. "Powerful, thoughtful, suspenseful...and compassionate."   John Gardner

IN EVIL HOUR, Gabriel Garcia Marquez   52167 $2.75
This exotically imaginative prelude to ONE HUNDRED YEARS OF SOLITUDE explores the violent longings festering beneath the surface of a South American town. "A celebration of life."   *Newsweek*

PICTURES FROM AN INSTITUTION
Randall Jarrell   49650 $2.95
The distinguished American poet Randall Jarrell lampoons a world of intellectual pride and pomposity. "One of the wittiest books of modern times."   *New York Times*

PASSION IN THE DESERT, Curt Leviant   76125 $2.25
In the majestic desert of the Sinai, a man embarks on an emotional odyssey, exploring the depths of his memory and passion.

MCKAY'S BEES, Thomas McMahon   53579 $2.75
Set on the eve of the Civil War, this is the comic story of one man's attempt to gain a fortune as he encounters love, sex, slavery, and ambition. "A delightful piece of writing."   *Los Angeles Times*

SECRET ISAAC, Jerome Charyn   47126 $2.75
A triumphant tale of villainy, true love and revenge set on the streets of New York. "SECRET ISAAC is a veritable Fourth of July."   *New York Times*

SEVENTH BABE, Jerome Charyn   51540 $2.95
A wildly comic novel that delivers a curveball vision of America's national pastime—baseball. "Strange and wonderful."   *New York Times*

THE EDUCATION OF PATRICK SILVER
Jerome Charyn   53603 $2.75
A wild and gutsy novel about big-city cops, crooks and freaks. "A lead-in-yer-liver cop story."   *Boston Globe*

Available wherever paperbacks are sold, or directly from the publisher. Include 50¢ per copy for postage and handling; allow 4-6 weeks for delivery. Avon Books, Mail Order Dept., 224 West 57th St., N.Y., N.Y. 10019

AVON Paperback

Bard 1-81

AVON BOOKS
BY JEROME CHARYN

THE SEVENTH BABE 51540 $2.95
A wildly comic novel that delivers a curveball vision of America's favorite national pastime—baseball. "Strange and wonderful...Charyn is one of our consistently daring and interesting writers." *New York Times*

SECRET ISAAC 47126 $2.75
An epic tale of crime and passion on the urban frontier, featuring Jerome Charyn's indomitable cop-hero Isaac Sidel. "SECRET ISAAC is a veritable Fourth of July." *New York Times*

THE EDUCATION OF PATRICK SILVER 53603 $2.75
Through the pornographic underbelly of New York First Deputy Commissioner Isaac Sidel stalks a renegade cop who has switched sides—and is now a bodyguard for a cut-throat leader of the mob underworld. "Charyn turns his tough-guy rhythms up full volume. A lead-in-yer-belly cop story." *Boston Globe*

THE FRANKLIN SCARE 41335 $1.95
Franklin Roosevelt's personal barber, Oliver Beebe lives in the attic of the White House, eats Baby Ruths, reads movie magazines, dines with J. Edgar Hoover and becomes the most intimate advisor to the most powerful man on earth. "Good lively fun." *Los Angeles Times*

Available wherever paperbacks are sold, or directly from the publisher. Include 50¢ per copy for postage and handling: allow 4-6 weeks for delivery. Avon Books, Mail Order Dept., 224 West 57th St., N.Y., N.Y. 10019

Charyn 1-81

BARD BOOKS
DISTINGUISHED DRAMA

Title	Code	Price
BENT, Martin Sherman	75754	2.50
BIZARRE BEHAVIOR: SIX PLAYS BY INNAURATO Albert Innaurato	75903	3.50
DREAM PLAY, August Strindberg	18655	.75
EDWARD II, Christopher Marlowe	18648	.75
EQUUS, Peter Shaffer	51797	2.50
FANTASTICKS, Jones/Schmidt	54007	2.50
FIVE PLAYS BY RONALD RIBMAN Ronald Ribman	40006	2.95
GAY PLAYS: THE FIRST COLLECTION William H. Hoffman, Ed.	77263	3.95
GETTING OUT, Marsha Norman	75184	2.50
GREAT JEWISH PLAYS Joseph C. Landis, Ed.	51573	3.50
HISTORY OF THE AMERICAN FILM Christopher Durang	39271	1.95
IMPORTANCE OF BEING EARNEST Oscar Wilde	50880	1.75
INSPECTOR GENERAL Henry Popkin & Nikolai Gogol, Eds.	28878	.95
LOWER DEPTHS, Maxim Gorky	18630	.75
MEMOIR, John Murrell	38521	1.95
MISS JULIE, August Strindberg	36855	.95
MISS MARGARIDA'S WAY Roberto Athayde	40568	1.95
PIPPIN Roger O. Hirson & Stephen Schwartz	45740	2.25
SEA GULL, Anton Chekhov	24638	.95
SHADOW BOX, Michael Cristofer	46839	2.25
UNCOMMON WOMEN AND OTHERS Wendy Wasserstein	45997	2.25
WAKEFIELD PLAYS, Israel Horovitz	42903	3.50
WHOSE LIFE IS IT ANYWAY? Brian Clark	52407	2.50

Available wherever paperbacks are sold, or directly from the publisher. Include 50¢ per copy for postage and handling; allow 4-6 weeks for delivery. Avon Books, Mail Order Dept., 224 West 57th St., N.Y., N.Y. 10019

AVON Paperback

BDD 1-81